THE SEVEN STAIR CREW
THE SINKHOLE

Brad V. Cowan

LORIMER

James Lorimer & Company Ltd., Publishers
Toronto

James Lorimer & Company Ltd., Publishers acknowledges the support
of the Ontario Arts Council. We acknowledge the financial support
of the Government of Canada through the Canada Book Fund for
our publishing activities. We acknowledge the support of the Canada
Council for the Arts which last year invested $24.3 million in writing
and publishing throughout Canada. We acknowledge the Government
of Ontario through the Ontario Media Development Corporation's
Ontario Book Initiative.

The Canada Council | Le Conseil des Arts
for the Arts | du Canada

ONTARIO ARTS COUNCIL
CONSEIL DES ARTS DE L'ONTARIO

Cover image: Shutterstock

Library and Archives Canada Cataloguing in Publication
Cowan, Brad V., author
         The sinkhole / Brad V. Cowan

(The Seven Stair Crew)
Issued in print and electronic formats.
ISBN 978-1-4594-0724-4 (bound).-- ISBN 978-1-4594-0723-7 (pbk.).
--ISBN 978-1-4594-0725-1 (epub)

         I. Title. II. Series: Cowan, Brad V. Seven Stair Crew.

PS8605.O924S53 2014   jC813'.6   C2014-903018-5
C2014-903019-3

James Lorimer & Company Ltd.,   Distributed in the United States by:
Publishers   Orca Book Publishers
317 Adelaide Street West,   P.O. Box 468
Suite 1002   Custer, WA, U.S.A.
Toronto, ON, Canada   98240-0468
M5V 1P9
www.lorimer.ca

Printed and bound in Canada
Manufactured by Friesens Corporation in Altona, Manitoba,
Canada in August 2014.
Job #205789

For JSC, the master map artist (and one heck of a dad)

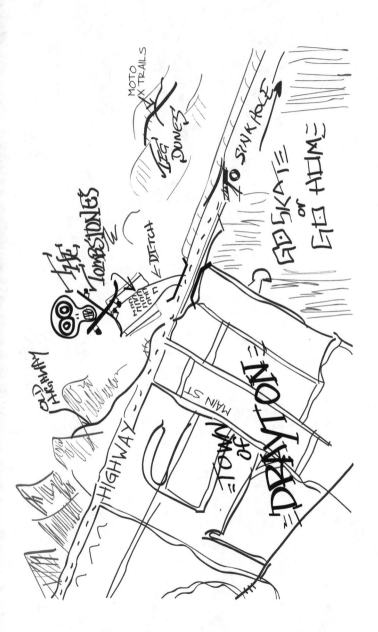

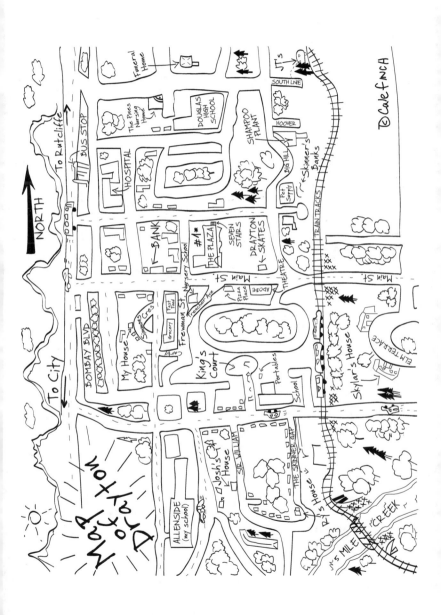

CHAPTER 1
SUMMER DAZE

It was the last day of school, and Cale's leg was shaking uncontrollably under his desk. He sat up, his back as straight as a board, his hot hands clasped together on the desk's lid. A small fan in the corner of classroom 7A buzzed away, doing its best to pump a little air across the backs of the seated students, but it was not enough. The room was stifling. The only thing the fan did do was blow the smells of Alberta's early summer into the classroom: scents like lilac and fresh grass clippings — things that reminded Cale of the season he loved most. He wanted to get the heck out of the classroom and on to his next skateboarding adventure. Cale was a skater after all, and when you spend most of your waking (non-school) life on a skateboard, everything is an adventure.

In spite of the heat, Cale was wearing a pair of his usual slim black jeans and a gauzy, lime-green crewneck T-shirt that had two buttons at the neck. His arms were thin, but wiry, and tanned from being outside as much as he was. It was his shoes though, that gave him away as a skateboarder. The outsoles of both, near the toe, were scuffed from constant and focused rubbing on the grip tape of his board. Every time he ollied or spun a flip trick, his shoes became more and more worn. The laces in both shoes had been retied a few times, too — victims of particularly intense ollies and constant attempts to perfect his three-sixty flips.

Cale was determined to be the first one out that door, the first one to his locker, where he would throw on his backpack, grab his skateboard, and be out of the building before anyone else. He wanted to be the one who had the first taste of the summer days ahead. He shifted in his seat, flicked his scruffy brown bangs out of his eyes, and began to drum his fingers on the scratched and graffiti-etched desk.

He shifted his eyes from Ms. Chin to the clock and then from the clock to Ms. Chin.

She finally lifted her eyes from the book she was reading and cocked an eyebrow in Cale's direction.

"You realize there are more than sixty days of

summer, don't you, Cale?" she said, smiling lazily. "Do you think nine extra minutes will really matter?"

Cale let out a sigh. "Actually, Ms. Chin, I really do."

She leaned back in her chair and set her book on her desk, just as a paper airplane flew over her head, hit the blackboard, and dropped to the ground.

"Carlos! No more of that!" she yelled, only half annoyed, in the direction of the class clown. Carlos immediately plunked his head on his desktop, let out a strange groan, and pretended to be dead.

"Humour me, Cale. What would you do with those extra ..." She gazed at the clock again. "Eight-and-a-half minutes?"

Cale took a deep breath. "First, I would grab my stuff from my locker, jump on my skateboard, roll out of school, ollie over the yellow curb at the side of the staff parking lot, and, since there would be no traffic to dodge, I'd be on the street in no time. With no other kids on the walking path to avoid, I could roll down that shortcut full speed, then do a kickflip out of the curb-cut on my street, and be at the door of my house to check the mailbox before any other kid was even out of their classroom."

Ms. Chin nodded. "Why do you need to get home so badly? Got a flight to catch?"

"No, I just, I gotta check the mailbox," Cale said. "It's really important."

"Report cards don't come out for another week, Cale. You do know that, right?" Ms. Chin said, like report cards were the most important things in the world.

"I don't care about my report card," Cale said. "I mean, I care about it. But that's not what I'm talking about. Unless I need to be worried about it?"

Ms. Chin shook her head and leaned a little closer to Cale. "I wouldn't be worried if I were you," she said in a half whisper.

Cale was a solid B+ student, and most of his teachers thought he was a great kid. The only exception was the vice-principal, Mr. Greig, who had caught Cale riding down the hall on his skateboard once, and every day since, made a point of shooting Cale a stink-eye.

"So, what are you expecting in that mailbox, if I may ask?"

"I have no idea. Just something from my dad. He lives in California," Cale said proudly. "I mean he used to live here, in Drayton, but now he lives in San Diego. I've never met him, but we talk on the phone sometimes. Last time we spoke he said he'd mailed me a parcel. I just, I think it's going to be there today. I mean, it's been almost two weeks.

That's why I'd appreciate a little, you know . . ."

"A little what?" Ms. Chin said.

"Can we go early? Please?" Cale said.

"Ladies and gentleman of 7A," Ms. Chin said, grabbing the attention of the rest of the class. "Cale Finch has asked if I'll dismiss you early."

Every head in the classroom turned toward the teacher at once. Like heads puppetted by the same hand. The room became completely quiet.

"Today may be the last day of school, but it's a day like any other day and there are still seven minutes of class left," Ms. Chin said.

Cale's shoulders sank as a chorus of groans oozed out of his classmates. He really thought she might let them out early. Instead he was forced to sit in the agony of anticipation, his leg still shaking under the desk.

In due course, the dismissal bell rang out, prompting Cale and the rest of his class to jump from their seats, cheering and whooping wildly as they bumped toward the front of the class.

"Have a great summer! And good luck!" Ms. Chin called out.

Cale heard everything but the "good luck." He had already escaped into the coolness of the empty hallway, silently dashing around the corner to his locker. Snapping it open with a deft flick of his wrist, he grabbed his skateboard by the nose, yanked it out, and leaned it on the locker beside his own. He slid on his backpack and pulled his baseball cap on, twisting the brim just slightly to the side. He looked left, deep into the empty hallway, then to the right, past the office, and toward the doors leading outside. Grabbing his skate, he ran a few steps, threw the board down, and jumped on it, rolling smoothly on the grey polished floors of the main hallway. Kids began spilling from other classrooms, but Cale was quick to dodge them as they shot weird looks his way.

A pang of worry leapt in Cale's chest as he quickly drifted past the office. "This is crazy," he thought to himself, knowing how risky it was to skateboard through the hallways of the school. "But it's the last day. What could possibly go wrong?"

Out of nowhere, Vice-Principal Greig stepped from the office and directly into Cale's path. He was carrying a glass jug of water and talking to someone over his shoulder. Cale carved his board to the left, going between Mr. Greig and the school secretary who stepped out of the office directly behind him. Cale got low on his board and somehow managed to sift past them without bumping into either. Mr. Greig, caught completely off guard, almost lost his balance and the water in the jug sloshed out and onto the floor. The secretary grabbed her chest like she was witnessing the most awful thing she'd ever seen and let out a dramatic gasp.

"No skateboarding in the halls, Cale! Off the board! Now!"

Cale kicked his board expertly into his hand, tucked it under his arm, and slipped past a group of younger kids cleaning out their lockers. Popping the crash bar on the door at the end of the hallway, he disappeared into the bright light of the afternoon.

Cale laughed to himself as he jumped back on his board, and, just as he'd planned, ollied the yellow curb, landing on a slanted section of dark asphalt that led to the staff parking lot of Allenside Elementary. It was the smoothest parking lot in the town of Drayton. He pushed a few times to gather speed, and then, turning back toward the school, gave it one last, hard look.

Sure, he'd probably skate past it a few times this summer, but then it would be empty. In this moment, he loved the feeling of being one of the first kids out of class. It made him feel like he was the first to escape, the first to really get a taste of summer. But it lasted only a moment. Flocks of kids were starting to pour out of the front doors, laughing, yelling, and running across the dry, yellow grass near the front doors. As they did this, they kicked up little clouds of dust.

"We need rain," Cale thought to himself, echoing what he'd heard his mother say every day for the last few weeks.

Something in a window on the second floor of Allenside caught Cale's eye in that moment. It was Angie. She was waving to Cale as a sea of students passed excitedly behind her. She had recently cut her long, straight brown hair into a boyish pixie cut, and Cale thought it made her look even more amazing. It brought out her brown eyes and pale skin. Cale waved back to her.

Back down on the street, Cale continued to pump his right leg harder and harder, piloting his board toward home. He hoped that Angie was still watching him, and he hoped she thought he looked cool.

He cracked a nollie over a sewer grate and zig-zagged around two yellow school buses parked against the curb. He arced a big turn toward the skinny footpath that snaked its way down a hill, cutting a cool line through the yellowed grass. The path was made of hard-packed dirt rather than asphalt or concrete. Months ago, Cale would have leapt from his board at this point and walked down the hill to the next bit of roadway, but recently, his buddy JT, the leader of Cale's "Seven Stair Crew" had shown him that the dirt was actually skateable. This seemed crazy at first. Cale didn't really understand the science of how little urethane wheels could still spin when they hit dirt, but somehow they did, and since the walkway twisted and turned downhill, he could also pick up some serious speed.

He rolled quickly toward the mouth of the trail and leaned his weight into his back foot. His board slowed a little when it hit the packed earth, but a moment later he reached the top of the first incline. Then gravity took hold, sucking him downhill, first curving slowly left, then right, and then through a small stand of pine trees. He ollied right out of a bump at the end and landed smoothly on the street below. Cale still had some good speed, so he set up his feet and popped a perfect heelflip over a discarded piece of Styrofoam that drifted into his path.

Cale did a backside one-eighty ollie over the bump at the bottom of his driveway and rode switch all the way up the grade of his driveway, slowing to a stop at the bottom of the rowhouse's concrete steps. He could see his mom's little blue car parked in the open garage. She'd left the trunk open, and the dome light inside was on. Cale just shook his head as he closed the trunk.

"Artists," he said with a sigh.

He bounded up the front steps and flipped open the tarnished gold mailbox. It was empty.

CHAPTER 2
THE EMPIRE

Cale slammed the storm door and kicked his shoes off in a huff. Plunking his bag down, he made his way into the kitchen where his mom was up to her elbows in something she was wrestling with in the sink.

"There he is!" she said in a singsong voice, lifting one of her plaster-covered hands out of the sink and wiping her brow. "How was the last day of grade seven?"

"Fine. It was cool, I guess. Nothing special. Did anything come for me today? In the mail?"

"Can you help me with this, honey?" she said, beckoning him toward the sink with a flick of her head. "My hands are just covered in this stuff."

Cale walked over and helped her wrestle a big slab of clay into a massive plastic tub.

"Let me have a kiss," she said, smearing her lips onto his forehead as he jokingly pulled away.

"You know, Mom, some kids get gifts when they finish a school year. Did you know that?"

"What do I always say?"

"You'll only get something if you don't pass!" they said together slowly, shaking their fists in mock violence.

"How's this for a gift?" she said, drying her hands on her apron and grabbing something from the shelf above the stove.

She plunked a plump manila envelope on the counter in front of him. "It's post marked 'San Diego.' I wonder who that could be from."

Cale grinned as he tore the envelope open.

Cale,

This is your captain speaking . . . joke. This is your dad, Lance. I'm looking out the window of my place at the beach, the waves, and Castro Point, one of the best surf spots in San Diego . . . Wish you were here, buddy.

Cale looked up from the letter. Sure enough, his mom had ducked back down into her basement studio. To give him some space. He could hear her humming to herself, but Cale knew that it was hard for her to see him getting close to his dad.

Well, here we go: another year over and a whole summer ahead.

First things first, as I promised you. Here are two of my old skate T-shirts. Kind of a fluke that neon pink and yellow are back this season, so you'll be in fashion (even though Fractured Skates no longer makes boards, and Drayton Pipelines went out of business years ago). Wear them with pride, though they might be a bit big on you.

So there you are. Done school for the year, and here comes the summer. If Drayton's still anything like it used to be, that place clears out as soon school's over. People go to their cottages, go camping, or just get the heck out of there. Man, I can remember being in that town during some of the hottest summers on record. If it weren't for the vert ramp we built behind the rec centre, those summers would have been bo-ring. We'd skate all day and swim in a friend's pool all night. The other thing that made the summers bearable, from a skateboard point of view, was . . . the Empire.

Cale flipped over the page quickly, where the letter continued.

The Empire wasn't (isn't) an arcade or record store

or skate shop . . . It was a series of three super-secret skate spots hidden in and around the town that only a very select few knew about. These locations were so top secret that only my crew knew of their existence. We were the only ones to "skate the Empire." As far as I know, we still are. I haven't told another soul about any of this. Until now.

So here we are. Now, since I'm pretty sure you're not going to come visit me anytime soon, I'd like to play a little game with you. A challenge, if you will. I am going to give you a clue to one of the spots. It's the easiest one to find, and it might just be the easiest one to skate. What you have to do is find it, skate it, and send me some kind of evidence. Maybe a picture, maybe a drawing, maybe a letter. If you can prove you were there, I'll send you a clue to the next location . . .

How about it? A little fun to make the summer less boring. A reason to stay in touch with your old man.

Here's the clue that will lead you to the first map:

*If you're ready to start the "Empire" quest
keep this envelope close to your chest.
A map to the "Tombstones" will begin the whole caper.
Just check on both sides of every paper.*

Love you, buddy. Enjoy.

Dad

Cale's heart thumped in his chest as he poured the contents of the manila envelope onto the kitchen table. Out tumbled the two bright, old-school skate shirts and a sticker that said "Drayton Pipelines," but that was it. He read the rhyming clue again.

"Both sides of every paper?" he said to himself, looking at the letter. "But there's only one piece of paper!"

Cale shoved his hand into the mouth of the envelope. Then he peered inside. It was empty. He took stock of the items again. The letter was one page, written on both sides. The T-shirts had nothing wrapped inside of them. And the sticker was exactly that: just a sticker. His mind raced. Quickly, almost instinctively, he peeled the backing from the sticker. But when the two pieces came apart, there was nothing written on either side.

Next, he ran to the toaster and turned it on. He'd seen a kid's detective show where someone had written some words, using lemon juice, that were invisible until heated. He watched the zig-zag elements inside the toaster reach their max and then stretched the page of the letter over the shimmering heat. He waited and waited, but it wasn't long before his fingers started to get too hot. No words were appearing. Cale pulled the paper back from the heat, but it was too late. The page had gotten so hot that a brown oval started to sear itself into the centre of the white page. The letter was catching fire!

Cale quickly blew out the flames, but not before a thumb-sized hole had burned its way through. Cale flipped the page over to where the riddle was written. Whew! It was still intact.

"Honey, what's burning up there?" his mom yelled from the basement. "Are you playing with matches?"

"No, Mom!" Cale shouted back, trying to sound as if everything was under control. "Just . . . uh . . . just a toaster malfunction."

"Well, if you're hungry," Cale's mom said as she bopped her way up the basement stairs, "maybe we should go out for tacos!"

Cale smiled. He loved Mexican food, and he loved going out to a little taqueria in Drayton called Jimenez Tacos.

"Well, I guess it could be cool to celebrate my last day of school," Cale said, rounding up the pile of loot his father had sent and checking everything again for the map.

"My feeling exactly," his mom said.

★   ★   ★

The next morning, Cale stuffed the envelope with the letter and the sticker into his backpack and grabbed his hat and skateboard from beside the door. He was wearing the bright pink "Fractured Skates" T-shirt.

"Oh my gosh!" Cale's mom said. "I remember that shirt."

"Fits me pretty good, huh?" Cale said, putting on a goofy face. Clearly the shirt was about two sizes too big, but he didn't care.

"Your dad sent you that, right?" she asked, crossing her arms. "That's one thing we didn't talk about at tacos last night, but I really wanted to. I was glad to hear all about your friend Angie, but we need to clear a few things up about your dad." She slowly walked toward Cale, ducking down to get to the same eye level as him. "Cale. Your father is . . ."

"He's what?" Cale said defensively.

"I just don't want him to let you down. That's all," she said. "He has a way of . . ." She searched for the proper words. ". . . disappointing people. Even the people he loves."

Cale looked down and picked at his grip tape. "You don't even know everything about him, you know," he said. "Did you know he's told me stuff he's never told anybody?"

"Cale, I just don't want you to get hurt."

"I'm not going to get hurt," Cale said, forcing a smile. "Don't worry."

CHAPTER 3
MAP #1

Cale leapt down the steps outside and onto his board. He ollied over the crack at the bottom of his driveway and out to his street, pushing and pushing until his leg was tired and he had enough speed to coast — and to think.

He closed his eyes for a moment and felt the heat of the day rising up from the asphalt. It felt amazing. On the inside of his eyelids, for a brief flash, Cale saw the face of his father. Then knocking around in his brain, he heard a piece of the recent exchange he'd had with his mother. He could hear her saying, "He has a way of . . . disappointing people." He opened his eyes just in time to see that he was about to crash into a curb at the side of the road. He whacked the tail of his board and lifted the nose for a hard turn to keep him on course.

He really wanted to get to the safety of his main hangout, where his favorite people in the world would be. He had to get to the Seven Stairs Plaza. Every weekend or holiday, and even after most school days when the weather was nice, Cale would hit up the Plaza. It wasn't just that the Plaza was an amazing skate spot with concrete benches and sets of stairs and ledges. It was because of who would be there: the Seven Stair Crew. His "boys," his closest friends and the four people in town (besides Angie and his mom) who knew him best.

As Cale's wheels growled over a rough section of Main St., the Plaza came into view.

First he saw the blond mop of hair belonging to Skylar, who stood against the wall, wiping scuff marks from one of his skate wheels. Sure, Skylar liked his skateboard to look as clean and polished as his wardrobe. But cleaning wheels was pushing it, Cale thought. As Cale rounded the bend, he could see Ryan lying on one of the benches, ducking out of the bright morning sun, drumming on his knees and singing, probably the lyrics to some whacked-out, made-up song. Ryan was the creator of his own language and the teller of weird jokes. Most of Ryan's jokes sounded like they should be funny, but they really only made sense to him. Cale and the rest of the guys figured that was sort of the point.

Then he saw Josh, peering into the viewfinder of his video camera, as usual, Seconds later, out of nowhere, JT appeared. He was rolling quickly toward the opposite end of the bench Ryan was on. With textbook form and finesse, JT popped a kickflip backside tailslide along the smooth surface. JT landed it effortlessly as Josh captured it all on video, but the rest of the guys hardly took notice. After all, JT almost never missed stomping his landings, even on the most technical tricks.

Cale snapped an ollie up into the Plaza and slapped a high-five with Skylar, then bumped fists with Josh, who looked up only briefly from reviewing his latest footage.

"School's out, home-dog!" Ryan yelled from the shady bench. "Nothing to do except sleep in, skate, and snaaarg! No more homework!"

"When have you ever done homework?" JT asked.

"Good point. Hey, Cale, nice shirt," Skylar remarked.

"Did they not have your size or something, homie?" Ryan added. "Or did you go into the store asking for a pink XXL T-shirt with a rip in the armpit?"

Cale, plunking down on the bench, opened his bag. "My dad sent it to me."

JT tugged at the back of the shirt to read the faded screen print. "Fractured Skates. What's that?"

"Old skateboard company. He sent me two shirts. The other one is even more dope," he said proudly. "He also sent me this." Cale pulled out the envelope.

"Hey, guys, come check this out," JT said, beckoning Josh and Skylar over to the benches.

Cale dumped the sticker and the letter out of the brown envelope and tossed the envelope behind his back. JT fingered the sticker while Cale read the letter aloud.

The guys hung on every word and looked excitedly at one another when he got to the part about the Empire.

They scanned the letter again, with Cale reading the best parts over, at their urging:

The Empire . . . was a series of three super-secret skate spots hidden in and around the town . . . so top secret that only my crew knew about them . . . I am going to give you a clue to one of the spots . . .

Cale gazed around the circle of guys. They were all staring at the letter except for JT, and his eyes were off in the middle distance.

"This is like some real-life detective deal," Ryan said. "Inspector stuff." Everyone looked at Ryan quizzically. "Espionage vibes," he added in a goofy voice.

"You are so whack, Ry," said Skylar. Then he turned to Cale. "Do you think this is for real or is your dad just playing some kinda game?"

"I think it's made up," JT said. "I know this town better than anyone. There aren't any skate spots that I don't know about."

Cale looked down at the ground and sighed. He knew that JT might be right. Again his mother's words about his father "disappointing people" echoed in his head.

"Read the clue again," said Josh, ignoring the others. Instead, he chewed the inside of his cheek thoughtfully.

Cale read it back. "Here's the clue that will lead you to the first map:

If you're ready to start the "Empire" quest

keep this envelope close to your chest.

A map to the "Tombstones" will begin the whole caper.

Just check on both sides of every paper."

After a pause, Josh asked, "Why is the page burned? Did it come like that?"

"No, I, uh, well, I burned it when I thought some secret words were written on it in lemon juice. I saw it on some dumb show." Cale winced.

"It's not a bad idea," Josh said, slowly removing the page from Cale's hand. "Let me take a closer look."

Josh mouthed the words from the clue silently to himself, scratching the back of his neck. "What came in the envelope?" he asked.

"Just this letter, two shirts, and a sticker," Cale said. "I already peeled back the sticker and there was nothing there."

"Why would your dad say he was sending a map and then not send one?"

Skylar asked, "Do you think maybe he forgot to put it in the envelope?"

Cale just shook his head and shrugged.

"He's just playing a prank," JT said. "A trick."

"Either way, it sucks," Ryan said.

Josh was still holding the letter. "Did you bring the envelope with you?" he asked.

"Yeah," Cale said, producing the large brown-paper envelope from behind his back. "Check for yourself. It's empty." He shook it upside down as proof.

Josh took the envelope and popped open the mouth of it as wide as he could. He held it up to his eyes and squinted as he peered inside.

"Looks pretty empty, bro," Ryan said, peeking over Josh's shoulder.

"No, it doesn't," Josh said. "JT, hand me your knife."

JT flipped his hair back, and from the front pocket of his jeans slid out a small pearl-handled pocket knife.

"What is it?" Cale asked as Josh slid the blade inside the envelope and began slicing along the fold.

"Well . . ." Josh said, as he rounded the corner and began cutting the bottom edge. "This . . ." he continued as he set the little blade down on the concrete and opened the envelope up as if it were a pair of wings, ". . . is a map."

CHAPTER 4
X MARKS THE SPOT

The hair on the back of Cale's neck stood up as his eyes darted about the inside of the envelope, now laid flat. Everyone in the crew jostled around for a better view of what Josh had uncovered.

Lines and words and arrows, written in soft pencil, covered the large page. With two simple cuts, Josh had turned an envelope into a map — a map to what looked like hidden treasure. And by the look on his face, he seemed pretty proud of himself for finding it.

Cale's eyes moved over places on the map he recognized — street names, roadways, bridges — but then they came to rest on something sort of eerie: a title at the top of the map that read "#1. The Tombstones."

"*Keep this envelope close to your chest*," Josh said. "That was the clue. Why else would someone keep an envelope?"

"You're lucky you didn't just toss this into the recycling bin," JT said, picking his knife up from off the ground.

Cale nodded in agreement and then looked back at the map, his finger tracking a line from the Plaza to where an X, made from hand-drawn skateboards, marked the spot, and "The Tombstones" was written again.

"Do you guys know where that is?" Cale asked, looking specifically at JT.

JT came in for a closer look. "Near the old highway, I guess. Near where my mom's ex-boyfriend took me dirt-biking when I was a kid."

"You mean the dunes?" Josh said.

"No, the dunes are farther up. This looks like it's right beside the old highway," Josh said.

"How long would it take us to skate there?" Skylar asked impatiently.

"Don't you mean how long would it take if your mommy drove you?" Ryan said in baby talk.

"Okay, there's no way I'm sharing a bunk with you at skate camp!" Skylar said. "You vibe me way too much. Anyway, she doesn't drive me that much."

Cale knew that Ryan and Skylar were headed out in a few days to one of those skate camps in the country. It was called "SkateRanch" and the two of them couldn't stop talking about it. Cale had seen pictures and videos of it on the SkateRanch website. It seemed to have every type of skate park and ramp possible, and a few top pros always made some guest appearances. It was also incredibly expensive, which is why Cale, Josh, and JT weren't going.

"Serious, how long would it take to get to these . . . tombstones? Whatever they are," Skylar asked again.

"It's about a forty-minute skate, give or take," JT said, "but when you get close to the highway, the roads are really sandy and covered with little stones."

Out of nowhere the sound of skate wheels echoed through the open-air Plaza.

"Geek alert, geek alert," said Ryan.

"Oh no," said Skylar.

"Toby," JT stated flatly. "Perfect timing as always."

Toby rolled off balance toward the guys. He held a multicoloured scoop of ice cream on a waffle cone in one hand.

"Hey, dudes," he said as he licked the melting ice cream off his wrist. "The freezer's broken over at the variety store. They're givin' away all the ice cream for nothin'."

"Really?" Ryan said. "For free?"

"Yeah, the only problem is it's practically all melted, so, snooze you lose," Toby said.

"Then why would you tell us about it?" asked JT.

"I don't know," Toby said, the goop from the cone now sliding off of his hand and splotching all over his grip tape. "What're you guys up to anyway? What's that?" he asked, eyeing the map.

"It's a map," said Cale. "My dad sent it to me."

"Ca-ale!" JT whispered fiercely. Toby was not a member of the SSC, but all of the guys knew he desperately wanted to be.

"What?" Cale said.

"Dude, he's a dorkfest."

"A map to what?" Toby asked.

"A map to your Granny's house," Ryan said.

"Aw, c'mon guys," Toby said, throwing the goopy cone in the trash and wiping his hands on his camouflage shorts. "Look, whatever. My dad just put new coping on the mini-ramp. You guys should come over and skate it. You wanna?"

"No, it's cool. But we might try to head out to a new skate spot. Wanna come?" Cale said.

JT threw his hands up, and jumped on his skateboard, beginning to roll around the Plaza. "Yo, Cale, can I talk to you for a second?"

Cale carefully finished rolling the map into a scroll and shoved it in his bag. He hopped on his board and rolled toward JT, snapping a tiny noseslide on the end of one of the benches he passed.

"Whatsup?"

"What's *up* is that you just invited the biggest loudmouth poseur in the whole town to a secret skate spot," JT said.

Cale's heart sank. He couldn't believe how careless he'd been about the information. It dawned on him that his father might be unimpressed.

"Do you think it matters? I mean, do you think he'll tell anyone?" Cale said anxiously.

"He's not part of the SSC. We know he wants to be, but do you really think he'll ever be able to ollie the seven?" JT said.

Ollieing the seven stairs at the Plaza was the "secret handshake," or rather, the "way in," to becoming a member of the crew. Cale had ollied the stairs only a few months ago and not without making a few disastrous attempts first.

"This whole Tombstones thing is crew business. If I had to vote, I'd say he shouldn't come," JT said.

Cale mulled it over. Toby was a nice kid and he loved skating, even if he couldn't handle his board. And Cale felt sort of bad for him. He knew what it felt like to be on the outside of the crew.

"It's my map," Cale said finally. "Let's let him come, just this once. We'll tell him to keep it a secret. If he doesn't, then he doesn't come with us to find the other spots."

"*If* there are any other spots," JT said.

"And what's with you being so negative about this whole thing in the first place?" Cale said, remembering JT's comments about the map being a prank a few minutes earlier.

"I'm still not sure it exists, even with that map."

"Only one way to find out," Cale said, straightening up and boldly staring right into JT's eyes.

Cale didn't know how to explain it, but he knew it wasn't a prank. Somehow, deep down in the core of his being he knew that it wasn't just a "game" either.

Cale knew his father was testing him, and this was a test he did not want to fail.

CHAPTER 5
DRAYTON CITY LIMITS

The next day, after breakfast, Cale raced on his board to Angie's house. He had overslept and was expecting the guys to meet him at his house in half an hour, but first he had to say goodbye to Angie.

As he zipped along the nearly empty streets, he couldn't help feeling that little pieces of his life were breaking away. Skylar and Josh were going to skate camp, and now Angie was going to her family cottage — not to mention the hundreds of kids from Allenside who seemed to just disappear at the end of school. Sometimes Drayton could feel like a ghost town in the summer, and Cale didn't love the feeling of being left behind.

Years ago, Cale's mom used to sign him up for swimming lessons or some "camps" when he was a kid — but those mostly just took place in hot gymnasiums and were more like school than he'd liked.

These days, all Cale wanted to do was skate.

As he pushed steadily toward Angie's, however, his mind zoomed away from the "left behind" feeling and toward the upside to this particular summer. This brand new quest for the Empire was one of the most exciting things that had ever happened to him. It held the promise of adventure and of heading out into the unknown — all in the name of skateboarding.

When Cale rounded the last corner and hit Angie's street, he could see her leaning back against her family's minivan. Her hands were behind her back, and she was sort of bouncing as she waited.

"Hey, Angie, sorry I'm late," Cale said, wiping the sweat from his forehead with the bottom of his shirt and kicking his board into his hand.

"That's okay," said Angie. "Just as long as I get to see you before we go."

"For sure," Cale said. "So you're gonna be gone the whole summer, right?"

"Pretty much. At least till the end of August," Angie said, looking down at her slip-ons and kicking a pebble away. "What's it like here in Drayton in the summer? I've never stuck around. We've always gone up north."

"Really?" Cale shrugged. "Well, it's dry, hot, boring, empty. Um, did I mention empty?" He sighed. "It's a bit weird sometimes, what with every-one gone. What's it like having a cottage?"

"It's fun. We swim. My older sister teaches canoeing, and sometimes we get to paddle over to this rope swing. It's super relaxing. I lie on the dock a lot, reading books."

"Sounds rough," Cale said.

"Hey!" she said, bopping him playfully on the shoulder with her fist. "I guess it gets kinda boring too. When it rains, it kinda sucks."

"You're just saying it's boring so I won't get jeal-ous," Cale said, smiling.

"Yeah, maybe. But sometimes I actually miss Drayton, and now that you and I are . . . well . . . you and I . . . I'm really going to miss being here. I'm really going to miss you."

Angie tugged Cale by the shirt sleeve and pulled him closer. Cale felt heat rush to his cheeks

"Quick, before my sister sees," she said, pos-itioning Cale so that her family minivan blocked the view of them from the house. She wrapped her arms around Cale and softly kissed his lips. Cale, caught off guard, didn't know what to do, so his arms just dangled by his sides. After a few seconds, Angie pulled away. "I'll see you in August. Okay?"

"Okay," Cale said, eyes buggy and left knee quaking.

"Oh, and I want you to have this," she said, removing a black rope necklace with a small charm on it and delicately putting it around Cale's neck. "It's a charm of St. Christopher. He's the patron saint of travellers."

"Why are you giving it to me? You're the one who's actually travelling somewhere," Cale said, holding the small circle of silver in the palm of his hand. He was surprised at how heavy it was for its size.

"Who knows? Maybe you will go somewhere this summer at some point," she said, sliding back around the van toward her house.

"Bye," Cale said. "See you soon."

Angie turned around and wiggled her fingers at him. Cale just stood there, still dazed by the magic of the kiss and still clutching the silver charm.

* * *

Cale rolled up to his house and ollied over the crack at the bottom of his driveway. In mid-air, his new necklace swung up and the charm whacked him right in the chin. It didn't hurt, but the surprise of it made him lose his balance and kick away his board. He saw all the members of the SSC relaxing under the small canopy over the concrete steps of his house, like a group of young lions ducking out of the heat and haze.

The boys were leaning forward to check out something playing on the flip-out screen on Josh's camera.

"Here it comes," Josh said, as they steadied themselves waiting for whatever was about to pop onto the screen. "And . . . *bang!*"

All of them screamed with laughter, clutching at each other for balance

Cale walked toward them as their giggles wore off. "Whatcha watching?"

"It's something that I filmed yesterday after you split. It's of —" Josh stopped, looking past Cale toward something or someone coming up the driveway. Cale spun around and saw a panting Toby leaning on his knees as his skateboard crawled to a stop.

"I'll show you later, man," Josh whispered conspiratorially.

"Dude, it's hot!" Toby said, pulling a massive blue plastic water bottle out of his backpack and taking a swig. Half of the gulp dripped down his chin onto his shirt, soaking his front. "Aw, man," he said, as the rest of the crew laughed at him. "Oh well, at least it's cooling me off!" He grinned at the group good-naturedly.

"Let's look at that map again," JT commanded. "Day's wastin'."

Cale retrieved the map from his backpack in the front hall and took it back to the guys on the driveway.

"Okay, there's the water tower — that's east out of town," Skylar said. "Wait . . . the water tower's there but not the subdivisions? Maybe we're looking at this wrong."

"My dad wouldn't know about those new houses," Cale reminded him. "Besides there's only one water tower in Drayton — that's got to be it."

"He's right," JT said. "Look at the highway, right where it curves. I know exactly where this is."

A drip of sweat rolled off JT's nose, right beside where the X was written. As soon as it fell, JT tried to wipe it away, but it was so hot that the droplet had almost immediately evaporated. "Let's roll," JT said.

The SSC with Toby in tow skated through the streets of Drayton, taking advantage of every curb, crack, and obstacle that came in their way. JT was out in front of the crew, snapping ollies and pop-shove-its with ease. Cale and Skylar, in the middle of the pack, were attempting long manuals, balancing only on their back wheels for blocks at a time. Next, Ryan and Josh pushed leisurely along, talking and joking, and occasionally staring over their shoulder where, quite a ways back, Toby huffed and puffed.

They skated down the mellow slope of a hill at the northeast end of town where the pavement got rough. Sand and dust pinwheeled in the small gaps between the road and the dead grass. At the end of the hill, the road became straight and flat for a section, then it curved, rounding tightly left, hugged by a metal guardrail. A large yellow sign that read "CITY LIMITS" stuck out of the ground behind the guardrail.

JT carved a few times in the flat at the bottom of the hill, dragging his foot to stop his speed before he hit the guardrail. Cale rode his board quickly till the last possible moment, before skillfully braking out a powerslide to stop himself only a few paces from the guardrail.

"Why are we stopping here?" Josh asked as the rest of the crew pulled in beside them.

"Shortcut," said JT. "We'll cut down this bike trail and over"

"Wait a sec," Cale said. "Where's Toby?"

As if on cue, Toby crested the hill, his wheels screaming under him, a look of absolute fear on his face. He was going way too fast. His board looked as if it was being driven by someone operating a remote-control device and trying to buck him off.

He was turning left and right, with no ability to influence direction or speed, or the fact that he was about to crash.

Cale's heart sank as he realized Toby was beyond help. Disaster was unavoidable.

Toby swerved radically before he hit the left shoulder of the roadway halfway down the hill. He and his board kicked up a cloud of dust as he flew, almost in slow motion, over the stone-flecked sand rise and out of sight.

"Oh crap!" JT said as the boys ran up the hill.

Toby was at the bottom of the rise, sitting in a soft pile of blow-sand looking dazed but calm.

"That was gnarly," Toby said with a smile.

"Dude, what happened?" JT said.

"You should have warned me," Toby said, standing up and brushing himself off. "I'm not that good on big hills."

★   ★   ★

Half an hour later, they were all standing at the end of the old highway as cars buzzed by them loudly on the new highway just beyond it. Cale studied the map as he tried to figure out their location.

"We're lost," Josh said. "Admit it, JT. You have no idea where we are."

JT just looked at Josh. "There's the water tower. This is the old highway," he said. "We may be a lot of things but we're not lost."

"Maybe the Tombstones were destroyed when they built the new highway," Ryan said. "Just guessing."

"Man, am I ever stupid!" Skylar said, pulling out a slick new smartphone wrapped in a bright orange case. "I have no idea why I didn't think of this before, but I have the BetterMaps app right here. Duh."

The guys stood and stared at Skylar as he shielded his eyes and peered into the screen. He scrunched up his nose, squinted, and held the phone slightly above his face.

"Can you pinpoint our coordinates?" Toby asked.

"Can you pinpoint the dork in the group?" Ryan said, mocking Toby.

"Forget you guys," Toby said. "I gotta take a leak anyway." Toby slouched off toward some sage grass up a small rise of sand beside them.

"Don't get eaten by a giant scorpion," JT said. "They always go for the weakest one first."

"Very funny," Toby said, turning his back to the guys and getting on with his business."

"Dude. Give it a rest." Cale scowled at JT. "Focus."

"Oh, man," Skylar said.

"What, no signal?" JT asked.

"No. I think it's overheated," Skylar moaned.

"Whoa, come here! You gotta see this!" Toby shouted from beyond the rise. "It's the Tombstones!"

CHAPTER 6
THE TOMBSTONES

The crew stood on the rise with Toby and surveyed the land in front of them. Sure enough, down a small levy and across a thick stand of tall grasses was one of the best skate spots they'd ever laid eyes on.

"The Tombstones," Cale said to himself under his breath, relieved.

The secret location that lay ahead looked like a dry riverbed made of concrete with two great slanted sides. The angled embankments were not steep, but long, and each was almost as wide as a highway. Hunks of concrete shot up from the smooth cement flat-bottom of this ditch; great slabs that looked exactly like headstones in a graveyard, only bigger.

Without a word, the crew trudged down the small hill and across the flats toward the skate spot. The wind blew the big stalks of grass back and forth, making them looking more like waves in the sea than dry plant life on a dusty flood plain.

"I get why they call this the Tombstones," JT said as he reached the top of the bank on the near side. "And check this out," he added. "Looks like someone added to the fun." JT slid his hand along the top of a parking block that someone had placed near the top of the embankment.

"Skaters must have moved this here," Josh said, filming everything he could, with his video camera's eyepiece pressed into his face.

Cale rubbed his hand on one that showed some skate-wear. "This one looks like it was waxed by other skaters a zillion years ago." He was right. There were the telltale slide and grind marks, but they were faded, almost to the point of being rubbed off. It didn't look like anyone had skated there in years. A shiver went up Cale's spine when he realized that the person who dragged the block there could have been his father.

"What's up, man?" JT said, grabbing Cale by the shoulders. "We found the place we were looking for, and now you seemed bummed."

"I'm not bummed, man. I'm just, uh, thinking." Cale said.

"Did you come here to think or to skate?" JT said, rolling down the embankment and picking up an enormous amount of speed. "Because I came to *skaaaate!*" He whooped as he rolled away from the crew and shrank in the distance. The rest of the crew watched in admiration as JT rocketed across the flat-bottom, weaving through the "tombstones," arcing a high turn on the far bank, and snapping an ollie. He carried his speed as he drifted back toward them and cracked a hardflip to fakie before rolling back down.

"C'mon!" he urged, his face glowing with excitement.

Cale went zipping down the one slope and up the other side. He tried a backside flip but lost control of his board and had to chase it down before it whizzed down the slope by itself. Jumping back on his deck, he rolled back down the bank and up the other side, where he locked into a feeble grind on the rough old parking block. His rear truck stuck, forcing him to jump off his board, which stayed lodged into the curb.

"This place is hard to skate," Cale muttered.

Everyone but Toby was rolling down one side and up the other, always trying tricks when they reached the apex of the bank. No one, with the exception of JT, was really able to pull off a trick.

"There's no flow," Skylar said, as he managed to work his board up to the top where JT, Josh, and

Cale were standing. "And those tombstones are so gnarly. Every time I'm rolling toward them, I get the feeling I'm going to smash into them."

"What do you think they are for?" Cale asked.

"I think it's to slow down the water before it goes under the highway," Toby said, from a few feet away from them. He was pointing at a large octagonal tunnel at the end of the ditch leading under the road.

"The water?" Cale asked.

"Flood water," Toby said, chewing a piece of long grass. "A big rain can create flash floods. The water rushes down the foothills, and it has to go somewhere. That's why the towns around here got so flooded last year. There weren't enough of these spillways."

"Right," Cale said, wondering how a place so dry would ever have to worry about filling up with water. It dawned on Cale that it hadn't rained in weeks.

"Speaking of water, man, I'm thirsty," Josh said. "Anyone bring any water?"

The boys' eyes drifted over to Toby, the only one with a backpack. All at once they remembered the huge blue water bottle that was inside.

"I did," Toby said, removing his backpack. "I got lots." But as he slid his backpack between his legs and removed the bottle, he noticed something. "Aw man, it spilled in my bag. Oh well, there's still some left." He immediately handed it to JT, who took a long pull, then passed it to Josh who took a more measured sip. Cale got it next and tried to take the smallest sip possible, but once it hit his tongue it was hard to pull away.

"*Eaaasy*, buddy," said Skylar, grabbing the bottle from Cale before he'd finished. By the time Skylar and Ryan had their way with the water, there was hardly any left. Toby, sitting on the ground, face still covered in dust, took the last remaining sip.

"Are you going to skate?" JT asked. "Or just sit there?"

"I told you, man. I'm not so good on hills. That's all this place is. Hills."

JT stared at Toby with a look of scorn. "What are you even doing here, kid?"

Toby looked back at JT, eyes wide. "That's not fair, JT," he said. "I try my best."

"I try my best," JT mocked.

"Hey, I'm the only one that brought water, which you guys were happy to drink. And if it weren't for me, you never would have found the Graveyard."

"You mean the Tombstones?" JT corrected, spitting on the ground at the top of the bank and rubbing it in with his shoe.

"Tombstones, Graveyard, same difference." Toby stood up.

"Dude, you are a living, breathing 'bail section,'" JT said, laughing. "Our crew is made up of good skateboarders, not guys who will drag us down." With that, JT rolled down the bank and up the other side, singing in a loud, punky voice that echoed through the concrete chasm.

The rest of the guys just stood there. Nobody said a thing. Cale shifted uncomfortably while Skylar looked down at his feet. Ryan and Josh just stared off into the distance.

Cale grasped at something to break the tension.

"Hey, Josh, maybe, uh, can you film me skating this?" Cale asked, tapping his foot eagerly. "I really want to show my dad that we were actually here."

"Sure, man," Josh said, grabbing his video camera. He flipped out the view screen and fumbled with a few controls. "Go for it," he said, hitting the red button.

Cale was determined to land a trick, regardless of how tough the spot was. Though it was far away, he could feel the camera on him, burning a hole in his back. He tore down the bank, then arced a turn up the far side and blasted back down, his wheels ricocheting their growl into the air as he passed one of the huge tombstone blocks. He had enough speed to carry his ride up the side closest to the camera, so with Josh rolling the video, he snapped a big frontside flip. He managed to control the board with his feet, catching the grip tape mid-rotation, and sticking the landing.

Cale came to a dead stop and hesitated for a second. He had landed the trick, but he still had to roll back down the steepest section. He held his breath as his momentum started to slowly carry him. Then gravity began to pull his weight down, down, down the bank, his bearings screaming, his eyes wide. He couldn't help but scream.

"*Yeoooooouwww!*" He yelled into the air as he reached the flat-bottom — wheels barking across the ground and a feeling of relief washing over him.

In the distance, he could hear his friends whistling and yelling in approval.

All Cale could think about was showing his dad the footage. In the back of his mind, he knew that he had passed the first test.

CHAPTER 7
PROOF

The next day, Cale was sitting in the coolness of Josh's basement, reviewing the footage from the Tombstones on Josh's computer.

More specifically, they were looking for the clip Cale wanted to send to his dad.

"Here it is, I think," Josh said, shuttling through footage in an editing program, then hitting the space bar.

Cale leaned forward to watch himself riding up the embankment, kickflipping his board frontside, landing clean, and rolling back down the bank.

"Boom," Josh said. "You nailed that."

"I need to send that to my dad," Cale said. "Just that clip. I need proof."

"Listen, man, I've got lots of footage of you from the video we shot. Want me to give that to you too?" Josh asked.

"No. I just need to show him that we made it to the spot. I need him to know we figured out his riddle," Cale said.

"Gotcha," Josh said. "But if you ever want any other footage, you let me know. You know, for, like, a sponsorship tape or whatever."

Cale had hardly even considered a sponsorship video, but Josh's words rolled around in his mind. Which made him think of something else video-related.

"Hey, Josh. What were you guys watching on my porch yesterday?" Cale asked. "It seemed like you didn't want me to see it."

"We didn't want Toby to see it," Josh said, smiling as his expert fingers scrubbed through the footage on his computer, looking for the clip in question. "Check this out." He hit the space bar, then cracked his knuckles and clasped his hands behind his head. "It's hilarious."

It was spy footage of Toby shot from far away. The camera zoomed in on the unsuspecting Toby as he rolled around the Plaza by himself. He half spun a kickflip, landed on his board trucks up, then fell awkwardly on his butt. Josh laughed, both on camera and in real life.

"This is the best part," Josh said. The video continued to play, with the camera zooming in on Toby

as he sat on the ground of the Plaza, looking defeated after the fall. A flock of pigeons drifted over
him. One of the pigeons let go of a huge white
dropping that landed square on Toby's shirt.

Cale tried to stifle his laugh as he watched the
scene unfold, but it was no use, he began giggling,
and the more he tried to stop, the more the giggle
bubbled up.

"You guys are so hard on Toby," Cale said, choking down the last of his chuckle. Now on the screen,
Toby was rubbing his shirt on the brick wall of the
Plaza, trying to remove the disgusting bird dirt and
making sure no one was looking. "It's not fair."

"Hey, you laughed too," Josh said. "He's hard on
himself."

"All he wants is to be part of the Seven Stair
Crew," Cale said. "I know exactly what that's like.
Feels like only yesterday I was in his shoes."

"There's a difference," Josh said, placing a USB
memory stick into Cale's palm. "You're a wicked
skater, and Toby isn't."

"Still, man, it's not fair," Cale said. "He may not
be all that great, but it doesn't mean we need to
make fun of him."

"But it's kinda fun," Josh said.

Cale couldn't believe it. He had always thought
of Josh as the most mature and thoughtful member

of the crew. To hear him talk and think like a bully was weird.

Cale tucked the memory stick in his front pocket and walked out of the basement.

"Thanks, Josh," he called down the stairs, and without waiting for a reply he grabbed his shoes and his skate and escaped from the house as fast as he could.

The sky was a vivid pink slashed with purple lines as Cale rode under it, picking up speed, racing down a small depression toward home. As his wheels thundered across the inclined asphalt, thoughts bounced around in his head. He kept thinking of two things: sending the footage from the Tombstones to his father and the video of Toby looking sadly hilarious.

After every ollie and every push of his board, Cale would pat his pocket to make sure the memory stick hadn't fallen out. He was pretty sure it wouldn't defy gravity and launch itself from his pocket, but still something nagged at his subconscious and made him check.

*   *   *

Later that night, Cale sat at the computer in his kitchen. His mom was playing opera music on the stereo, and she hummed to herself as she washed her paintbrushes at the sink. Cale kept looking over his shoulder, hoping that she wasn't spying on him as he wrote an email to his dad. He knew she didn't like him making contact. More importantly, he knew it hurt her a bit.

He tried to keep the email as generic as he could:

hey, man,

guess what? we figured everything out. everything. we found the map and tracked down the tombstones. sending you proof.

it was gnarly and pretty hard to skate but managed to get a trick on video.

looking forward to whatever comes next.

cale

When his mom bobbed back down to the basement, he used the opportunity to type his dad's email into the address field. Just as he was about to hit SEND, his mom poked up from behind him. He froze.

"Whatcha working on?" she asked.

Cale wanted to wrap his arms around the computer screen and block her view. In that instant he knew it would be too obvious.

"Just sending out a video," he said, faking a yawn and a stretch, and hoping that his arm was in the right position to block her view.

"Can I see it?" she asked.

"It's not really ready," Cale said. "It's just a clip Josh and I are working on."

She looked at him, let out a sigh, and then smiled. "I am so proud of you," she said. "I know, I tell you all the time, but imagine being me. Imagine how proud you'd be to be in my shoes."

"Please, Mom," Cale said, feeling caught between the weight of guilt and the fear of being found out. "It's just skateboarding. It's something I like. Look at you — you're an amazing artist."

"But I went to school for art. I had classes, lessons. You've never had one lesson. You did this all by yourself." She hugged him in close, then kissed him on the forehead.

"Mom," Cale said, as she turned to walk away, "nobody really takes skateboard lessons." She smiled and headed back toward the basement.

Cale spun in his chair, jammed the memory stick into the side of the computer, and dragged the clip onto his desktop. He quickly attached it to the email and watched the status bar slowly creep toward completion.

After what felt like five minutes the clip had attached itself to the email. Cale let out a huge breath and hit SEND.

CHAPTER 8
THE TOBY SESSIONS

Cale lay in bed, staring at the ceiling, unable to get comfortable in the heat that had plagued Drayton since mid-June. His mind flashed with daydreams and random images, eventually landing on skate tricks he wanted to learn. He imagined every trick he could think of, even going as far as drafting a sort of mental chart of tricks he could versus couldn't land.

Then he thought of Toby. He thought of Josh's secret filming; he remembered how he'd laughed at it. It made him feel awful. Cale pictured Toby at home, eating dinner with his family. He could see Toby's dad, Russ, his mom, Joanne, and his sister, Susan. He tried to think of the conversation they might be having. He pictured Russ asking Toby about skateboarding: tricks he was learning, how he was "fitting in" with the crew. Cale imagined Toby faking a smile, nodding as he picked at his food, even lying about his place in the group. But Cale reasoned that on the inside Toby would be feeling pretty cruddy

At that moment, Cale was struck with a radical idea that actually made him sit up in bed.

What if he helped Toby? What if he could give Toby some kind of edge? Could he train him? Teach him? Cale imagined himself as a kind of skateboard sensei. He couldn't just let Toby be the butt of jokes and an "almost" member of the crew. Cale decided that he was going to do something about it.

He flipped his pillow over to the cooler side and lay back down. Feeling good about his decision, he drifted off into a dreamless sleep.

★   ★   ★

The next day, Cale sat in the sunshine on his skateboard at the end of Toby's ink-black driveway. He'd already rung the doorbell twice and nobody had answered.

He jumped on his skateboard, and in the middle of the smooth driveway, he practised his inward heelflips to help him pass the time. The nollie inward heel was one of the few tricks Cale still had not learned properly. It was such a hard trick, not only because it was almost impossible to pop and spin, but also because it was easy to land the wrong way. To land "Primo" — meaning to land with the board on its side — was as painful on the feet as it was incredibly frustrating.

Cale reasoned with himself before every attempt, thinking about where he was distributing his weight, how he was popping the trick, and what would make the spin happen faster. He changed his stance slightly and hung his toes off the side a touch, allowing his heel a greater grip on the deck.

Then Cale did something that he always did when he was trying to land a tough trick: He visualized himself doing it perfectly. He closed his eyes and pictured what it would look like, as if his mind were a slow-motion camera shooting from across the street. He pictured the pop, the board spinning exactly how it should, and he pictured himself rolling away as if it was nothing. Before he tried the trick again, he had almost convinced himself that he had already pulled it off.

It worked. On his next attempt he finally kicked a perfect inward heelflip in the air. He watched the board spin in slow motion below him, arcing perfectly, as if he had done it a million times before. His landing wasn't perfect — he had leaned back too far and landed on the tail — but he was excited that he had done the tough part. Now he knew it could be done. It made him almost giddy with excitement. Before he could try another, he heard a little honk from a car's horn. It was Toby's.

Cale shielded his eyes from the scorch of the sun. He could see that Toby's mom was driving the family car, an old blue station wagon with bits of rust running along the side, and Toby was in the back seat. Cale waved. As the old beast lurched to a stop, a hubcap from one of the rear tires rolled off and hit the aluminum of the garage with a bang.

Toby jumped out of the car from the back seat, excited to see Cale but also a bit embarrassed.

"We're getting a new car, like, super soon," Toby said.

"Your dad has to get that raise he keeps talking about first," Toby's mom said, wrestling with the hatchback trunk. "Give me a hand, will ya?"

Toby reluctantly walked to the rear of the car, where his mom loaded his arms with a huge paper bag full of groceries.

"Can I help?" Cale asked, quickly moving to the back of the car.

"You don't have to, man," Toby said, holding his breath and gripping the bag as he shuffled his feet up the driveway, trying to get inside before spilling the contents.

"Thanks, Cale," Toby's mom said as she placed a smaller, less full bag in Cale's arms.

Inside the house, Cale followed Toby's lead and plunked the bag on the worn wooden kitchen table.

"Thanks, man," Toby said, sweating. "I think you saved me a load."

"I've got an idea," Cale said, as they walked through the storm door toward the front of the house. "I wanted to know what you thought about it."

They stopped on the grass out front. Cale sensed some hesitation on Toby's part and, for a moment, second-guessed his idea. But he jumped right in anyway.

"What would you think if we, uh, like, worked on tricks together?" Cale said, softening his idea slightly. "I mean, what if I helped you learn some tricks?"

"For real?" Toby said. "This isn't some Seven Stair Crew joke?"

"For real," Cale said. "You can help me with stuff just as much as I can help you."

Toby rolled his eyes. "Dude, you're amazing. You got second place in a contest that I wasn't even good enough to enter."

"Who cares about that?" Cale said. "What's important now is that we get you to be part of the crew."

Toby stood there, wide-eyed. "When do we start?"

"How about right now?" Cale said, walking toward his skateboard and kicking it into his hand.

Once Toby ran in to get his own board, the two boys rolled around the cul-de-sac, with Toby riding beside Cale. Cale popped an ollie, and Toby did the same. It wasn't as high or as stylish as Cale's, but it was a proper ollie.

"Nice, man," Cale said. "You've got ollies down. Now let's take it over something."

Toby looked keen as he pushed with new energy to keep up with Cale. Cale looked back and smiled. The teaching was going better than he'd expected.

"When you are going to ollie over something," Cale called over his shoulder, "don't concentrate on the object, but look ahead . . . look at the landing." He popped easily over a rough, steel-studded manhole cover.

Toby tried to do the same, but at the last minute before takeoff, he kicked his board away.

"Cale, I can't," Toby said. "I'm afraid of what will happen if my wheels land on top. I don't want to fall."

Cale deftly spun a turn and rolled back to Toby. "I don't want to fall either. Just try what I said. You can do it."

"But I've never done it before. How am I just suddenly going to do it?"

Cale rolled to a stop. It was hard to argue with Toby's logic. Cale took a breath and tried to explain. "You have to sort of trick yourself."

"What?" Toby said. "Trick myself? But I know I can't do it. I can't all of a sudden just trick myself into believing I can."

"Let me give you an example," Cale said. "Before you and your mom came home, I was trying some nollie inward heels. I had never done them before and they seemed impossible."

"So?" Toby said.

"So, I pictured myself doing it. I mean, I imagined that I *already could* do it," Cale said.

Toby wasn't convinced. "But I'm afraid of bailing. Remember when I flew off the road the other day? That wasn't exactly fun."

"Promise me you'll ollie this again," Cale said, pointing at the rusty metal lid. "And promise me you'll think only of *landing* it — not about falling."

Toby sighed and looked skyward. "All right," he said.

He rolled away from Cale, halfway down the cul-de-sac and tick-tacked his board so that it was pointing at the manhole cover. He took two solid pushes, jumped on his board, and locked his feet into an ollie position — front foot slightly back from the bolts and his back toe dug into the tail.

With perfect timing, Toby snapped his back foot down, lifting the board skyward, levelled it off with his front foot, and landed well beyond the manhole cover he was trying to clear.

"Yeah!" Cale yelled. "Nice!"

Toby's eyes bulged. "Whoa!" he breathed. "That was . . . that was . . . really easy!"

"I'm not going to say 'I told you so', but, yeah . . . I told you so."

"Now I want to ollie something else," Toby said, stoked.

Cale grabbed a discarded pop can from the gutter and stood it up. Toby promptly piloted his board toward it and ollied it with ease.

There was a look of sheer joy on Toby's face that spread to Cale. "Dude, that was the highest I've ever seen you ollie," Cale said.

"Now can we move on?" Toby asked. "'Cause I think I'm ready for kickflips!"

CHAPTER 9
TOBY'S FIRE

For the next few days, Cale started his mornings by heading to King's Court and working with Toby. He taught Toby how to pop kickflips, backside one-eighties, half-cabs, fakie ollies, and fakie flips. Toby wasn't a fast learner, but he was committed to practising and had, perhaps more importantly, overcome his fear of falling. Cale loved watching Toby's confidence soar upon landing a tough trick.

After zipping home to check the mail and sharing a quick lunch with his mom, Cale spent his afternoons with JT and Josh at the Plaza — playing games of S.K.A.T.E., trying to film tough ledge tricks, and talking about the next "secret spot" in the Empire.

"Ryan and Skylar are so lucky. I'll bet they're swimming at camp right now," JT said.

"Yeah, with a bunch of cute girls," Josh added.

"Nah, just wait. Those guys are going to miss out huge when we find the next Empire site," Cale said with more confidence than he felt, talking about the Empire as if he knew where the next map would lead. As if it were a fact. The reality was much different. Cale had not heard back from his dad. Not even an email response to Cale's trick at the Tombstones. A map at this point seemed unlikely, but Cale didn't tell them that.

Another thing Cale didn't tell the guys about was his morning sessions with Toby. For two reasons: For one, he wanted the timing to be right. In the daydreaming part of his mind, Cale pictured a scene where Toby would improve so much that he'd show up one day and blow JT's and Josh's minds. But Cale knew this was a very unlikely scenario. The second reason was that he was worried about what they would think. Like maybe his hanging out with a weaker skater would rub off on him. Was it even possible that Cale's skating was fading? Was that even a thing?

Cale thought the best and most realistic way of changing JT's mind was to keep working on the basics with Toby. Then, if Cale could convince Toby to actually attempt an ollie down the seven stairs — and if by some miracle Toby actually landed it — Toby would have to be admitted entrance. JT and the rest of the crew would have no other choice.

Cale certainly knew there were hurdles — one of which was that Ryan and Skylar would need to witness it. But Cale figured if he took a few more days with Toby and worked with him on his ollies, he might be able to make it happen.

★ ★ ★

That Thursday, nearing the end of a long week of skating, as the shimmering heat of the morning reached its peak, Toby surprised Cale by landing a kickflip over the manhole cover.

"Nice!" Cale said, bumping fists with Toby as he rolled past.

"What do you think the rest of the guys are going to say about us skating like this together?" Toby asked, wiping the sweat from his forehead.

Cale said nothing. Instead he picked up a smooth round stone from the road and marked a straight line across the dry, hot asphalt. Then he took three large paces past the line and drew another line parallel to it. The little rock worked well. The lines were clearly visible, almost as good as if Cale had used a piece of chalk.

"If I were you, I'd concentrate on what the guys are going to say when you become part of the SSC," Cale said.

"Yeah, right." Toby shrugged and pointed to the lines. "What's that for?"

"That," Cale said, tossing the stone away, "is the distance you need to clear if you want to ollie the seven."

Toby stepped off his board and let it roll by it-self to the curb. He stared at Cale suspiciously and wrinkled his nose.

"I think it would send a message that you were serious about being part of the crew, if you at least tried to ollie the seven," Cale added.

Toby walked over to his board and stepped back on it, floating toward the two lines, letting his board drift over them as he looked down. He spun a kick turn and came back, rolling over the expanse again.

"It's not actually that far," Toby muttered to himself. "Do you really think I can do it?"

"It doesn't matter what I think," Cale said. "What matters is what you believe."

"I'm going to do it," Toby said, looking at Cale with a fire in his eyes that Cale hadn't seen before. "I'm going to freakin' do it."

"Remember, you'll have a way crazier land-ing at the actual set of stairs, but this is about the distance you need to cover," Cale called to Toby, who was pushing away from the artificial gap. "And you'll need speed."

Toby gave a thumbs-up, his back still to Cale. He didn't even turn his head.

Cale stepped back on his own board and rolled away from the lines. He didn't want to distract Toby from the task at hand. Toby pushed his board quickly toward the two skinny white lines. After four huge pushes, Toby jumped back on his deck and prepped himself in the ollie position, feet perfect and knees bent — now just a few feet from the first marker.

At that moment, Cale crossed his fingers.

Toby's ollie was low, but he had a great deal of momentum, just enough to carry him over both lines. He landed cleanly, but his speed forced a wobble into his board, and he lost control. He tried to regain it for a moment but then lost his footing. Averting a massive bail, Toby managed instead to heave himself onto a piece of lawn just beside the road. He skidded on his knees, then his hands. He looked up toward Cale, thrilled.

"I did it. I did it!" he gasped. "I can't believe I did it!"

Cale rolled toward him, nodding in approval.

"Dude!" Toby said, popping to his feet, revealing rich green grass stains on the knees of his jeans. The fire was still burning in his eyes. "I can do it!"

CHAPTER 10
EVERYTHING EMPTY

That night, a strong, warm wind whipped through Drayton as Cale slept fitfully. His house creaked, and the small poplar trees outside the windows whistled mockingly. He never fell into the restful deepness of sleep he so craved. Instead, his mind imitated the wind and blew crazy thoughts around his head like so many dry leaves. Most of his thoughts were about his dad. Maybe his father didn't care about him and was toying with him like he was some dumb kid. Why hadn't he heard from his dad? Not even a reaction to the video clip? Nothing.

Cale dreamed of a crowd and pictured his father moving through the throngs of people. Cale chased him, knocking into people, unable to keep up. Finally Cale got close enough to yank his father by the sleeve, spinning the man around to face him. Cale was, for the moment, relieved.

"Dad, it's me. It's Cale," he said.

"Cale?"

"Your son, from Drayton," he said, feeling himself weaken.

"I don't have a son," said the man, as he pushed back into the thick, faceless horde.

Cale kicked his feet in his bed and woke up. His heart was beating double-time, and he sucked in a long slow breath to counter the effects of the dream. Rubbing his eyes, he saw the red numbers of his clock glowing in the dark: 2:17.

Cale plunked his head back on the pillow and tried to get back to sleep as the wind continued to shriek in little whistles through his neighbourhood.

★　　★　　★

"Are you getting up or not?" Cale's mom said in a singsong voice. "Or were you up all hours reading your skate mags?"

"Did you hear the wind last night?" Cale asked, bleary-eyed, edging himself up onto his elbows.

"Sure did. I think we even lost power," she said, motioning with her head toward Cale's small alarm clock.

Cale looked at it as it flashed 7:40, 7:40, 7:40 . . .

"Shoot. What time is it anyway?" Cale asked.

"It's almost ten-thirty," she said. "The mail's even come." She tossed a postcard onto Cale's bed.

He picked it up quickly and stared at the picture on the front, of two women lying in the sun in modest bathing suits and horn-rimmed sunglasses. The shot looked like it had been taken fifty years ago. The edges of the card were worn, and the whole thing had the look of being totally vintage. He flipped it over but there was nothing on it except for Cale's name and address and a series of odd-looking stamps.

"It's blank," his mom said.

It was too early for Cale to start thinking too hard. He knew he needed to meet up with Toby. It was already an hour and a half later than their normal meeting time.

"I gotta go, Mom. I'm late," Cale said, pulling on his jeans and rifling through his dresser for a clean tee. He pulled one on, leaned in and hugged his mom, and bolted from the room.

"One question," his mom said, following him into the hall. "Who's sending you blank postcards from Australia? And whatever for?"

"What?" Cale asked, turning to see his mom fanning herself with the antique postcard. He ran back to her and slid it out of her hand, "Good question," he said — and he meant it.

Cale pushed his board as fast as he could direction of King's Court, feeling a pang of h ...ger in his empty belly. As he rounded the final corner, he hoped to see Toby on the street waiting for him. No such luck.

Cale rapped on the front door of Toby's house but nobody answered. He poked his head over the fence in the back. Nothing, unless you counted the old, sketchy mini-ramp that Toby's dad had built.

For a moment, Cale was at a loss. Where could Toby be? Cale turned on the garden hose at the side of the house and took a long drink of cold water. After cranking the faucet off, Cale strode to the front of the house and surveyed the street again. Still empty.

Then a thought popped into his head that shook him. "What if . . ." Cale said aloud. "Oh no." Cale jumped on his board and zipped as fast as he could toward the main street of town.

Cale hoped he was wrong. He hoped that Toby was just grocery shopping again, but he knew somehow, deep down, that Toby had ventured to the Plaza alone.

Cale ollied up the curb at the edge of the Plaza and rolled onto the smooth surface within. It was empty too.

Then a sound echoed through the space. The hiccup-wail of an ambulance's siren. Cale straightened up. He could hear voices coming from the direction of the seven stairs. Cale hesitated for a moment, but then, sliding his board out in front of him, he stepped on it and drifted close to the top of the stairs, afraid of what he might find.

The scene was like something out of some bizarre dream. Toby sat on the grass, head tilted back, while one of guys who worked in the Plaza's sandwich shop talked on his cellphone. The guy was also holding what looked like a small bag of ice to Toby's ankle. Josh was videotaping the entire scene. He now panned the camera up to Cale on the top step.

"What happened?" Cale asked, fearing the worst.

"Poseur-boy broke his ankle. Or at least sprained it," JT said quietly from behind Cale. JT brushed by Cale, bounced down the stairs, and delivered a bottle of water to Toby, who thanked him. Toby smiled at Cale.

"Cale, you missed it!" Toby grimaced. "I tried the seven."

The ambulance bumped right up on the sidewalk. Two paramedics got out, pulled on rubber gloves, and checked Toby out. The guy from the sandwich shop stood up and walked back up the seven stairs shaking his head.

"Kids. So stupid, you guys," he said in a heavy accent. He threw the dripping bag of ice into a garbage can beside Cale. "Like you are crazy."

Cale wasn't sure who he was talking to, but his words seemed fitting, considering the circumstances. "What happened?" Cale asked, walking slowly down the stairs.

"I just went for it!" Toby groaned, as the paramedics helped him into the back of the ambulance.

Cale ran and grabbed Toby's board and handed it to him just before the doors closed.

"It was gnarly!" Toby said, eyes wide, as the back doors slammed shut.

Josh, JT, and Cale watched as the ambulance sped away, rounding the corner and flipping its flashing lights back on. As it disappeared, they could hear the squelch of the siren fire on again.

"I should have been here," Cale said.

"You missed it, but don't worry, I've got the footage," Josh said. "It's hilarious. You gotta see it."

"Shut up," Cale said. "When did you become such a jerk?"

"What?" Josh stared at him.

"You think this whole thing is funny?" Cale snapped.

"Don't worry," JT said soothingly. "His mom is meeting him at the hospital."

"Don't worry?" Cale said. "It could have been worse. I just don't understand why Toby getting hurt is all of a sudden so funny."

"Hey, you laughed when I showed you that other video," Josh said defensively.

"That was different," Cale said. "I knew he wasn't hurt."

"Hey, he was the one who wanted to try the stairs," JT said, shrugging. "We didn't force him."

"To see you guys like this . . . it sucks," Cale said, and he turned to walk away.

"You know what would have sucked even more?" JT called after him. "If Toby had landed it. Then we'd be stuck with him."

"What is wrong with you?" Cale asked, stepping back toward JT.

"Cale, what don't you get? If we let just anyone be part of the crew it'll mean no one will respect us."

"Respect?" Cale fumed. "What do you guys know about that? Respect. You've lost mine."

"Easy, Cale. Listen to JT," Josh pleaded. "We need to set the bar, make it tough to join."

"How's this sound? I don't want to be part of the crew anymore. I'm out," Cale said, his body shaking. He stormed out of the Plaza, this time without looking back.

*　　*　　*

When Cale got home, he plunked onto the coolness of the leather couch in his living room and flicked around the channels on TV. He wanted to tune out, forget about what had just happened. He'd spent so much time and energy wanting to be part of the crew, and in one hot-headed moment, he had quit. It was a radical move, something Cale had never expected he would actually do, but in the moment he had felt like it was the right thing to do.

After he'd surfed around for an hour or so, he stood up and stretched.

That's when the postcard fell out of his pocket.

He had forgotten all about it, but now he picked it up and looked at it with new eyes. He looked deeper into the photo of the women in the bathing suits, where he saw little pastel houses and a sign that said "The Desert Mirage." He flipped the card over again. Blank. He slid his thumb over the Australian postmark.

He swiftly made his way to the computer in the kitchen and logged into his email. His heart leapt when he saw the message from his dad in his inbox.

He clicked it open.

Saw the video. Very impressed. You get an A for effort.

A *is for Australia, where I* B.

Which explains the radio silence from me.

Surf trip to Bells Beach.

You get the postcard?

Stay tough out there. The desert isn't for the weak.

Though the email was brief, it excited him. He read it over a few more times. It dawned on him that perhaps the postcard held more secrets than he had first assumed. He sat back in his chair and smiled. Then he leaned forward toward the screen and wasted no time.

He searched "the Desert Mirage Australia" but nothing came up that made any sense. He looked at the postcard again. The smiling women by the pool in the picture seemed to be mocking him.

"What are you hiding?" he asked. He flipped the card over one more time and saw tiny print dividing the card. The print was so small it looked like a solid line. But when he squinted he could see it was, in fact, words. Rummaging around a desk drawer he found a small ruler with an even smaller magnifying glass built in. His hands shook as he laid the ruler over the card, setting the bubble of the magnifying glass over the tiny words. He sounded them out as he read them. "Bathers at the mineral baths, The Desert Mirage, Indian Springs, 1958."

Something rang a bell with Cale. Indian Springs. He had heard those words together before, but he couldn't remember where.

Quickly, he typed just "Indian Springs" into the search engine. The results popped up instantly. His eyes bulged and a shiver rolled through him.

The Desert Mirage wasn't halfway around the world. According to the top article, the Desert Mirage was just south of Drayton, in Indian Springs. Compared to Australia this was practically his backyard.

Next, Cale searched for a map of Indian Springs, but the satellite images of the area were blurry. He could, however, make out a smudged area a few miles away from Drayton, just off a dirt road next to the words "Indian Springs."

He zoomed back out to get the name of the dirt road, but nothing appeared. This nameless dirt road ended abruptly, in the middle of nowhere.

"Stay tough out there," Cale said to himself. He knew finding this second location, in the heat of the unforgiving land outside of town, was another test.

CHAPTER 11
DESERT MIRAGE

The next day, Cale packed his backpack full of granola bars, a big jug of water, and an extra T-shirt. He had printed out the map to Indian Springs, which he tucked deep into a zipped pocket on the bag. He looked at his watch. It was 9:15 a.m. Part of him was excited to go it alone, part of him was scared of what lay ahead.

"Mom," Cale called into the basement. "I'm going skating." He closed his eyes, hoping she would call back with a "see you soon," but instead, she climbed up the stairs to say goodbye in person.

"Will I see you for lunch?" she asked.

"No, I'm . . . um . . ." Cale thought about lying, but his conscience got the better of him. "I'm actually kind of going on a hike."

"A hike?" she asked. "What kind of hike?"

There was a knock on the door. Cale was happy

for the distraction, but less happy when he opened it. It was JT.

Cale opened the storm door to let JT in. "Hey, man," Cale said with a sigh.

"Are you going on the hike too?" Cale's mom asked.

"I don't know," JT said awkwardly, glancing at Cale. "Am I?"

"Wherever you go, stick together," Mom said, smiling. "And drink lots of water. It's hot out there."

"I got it covered, Mom," Cale said.

Cale grabbed his skateboard and waved to his mom.

"You're home for dinner, right?"

"Yup, for sure," he said.

Cale practically pushed by JT on his way out of the house, but JT was quick on his heels. Cale jumped on his board; JT trailed just behind. For the first few blocks Cale considered making a bolt for it. He didn't want to see JT, let alone share his adventure with him.

Cale kicked his board to a stop when he reached the edge of a street and waited for the light to change.

"Is there a reason you're following me?" Cale asked, not really looking for any kind of answer.

"Yeah, homie. I came by your place to say I'm sorry," JT said.

"Sorry for what?"

"Look, I don't want you to leave the crew," JT said.

"I don't want to be part of a crew of bullies," Cale said.

"I know we took it too far," JT said.

"I'll say," Cale snapped. "What is wrong with you guys? So what if Toby's not a great skater. He's working at it — and he's getting better."

"I know. I know," JT said. "I even saw him land a fakie flip. Impressive."

"Then you pressured him to try the stairs?" Cale quizzed.

"No," JT said. "Like I told you, he wanted to try it. I even tried to talk him *out* of it."

"Seriously?" Cale asked.

"Seriously," JT said, squinting in the bright sun. "Now, can you please tell me you didn't mean it — about quitting the crew?"

"As long as you promise that you're done being a jerk to Toby," Cale said.

"Done," JT said.

Cale stared at JT for a long while, sizing him up. JT just stared back.

Finally, Cale thrust his hand out, and JT shook it firmly.

"Now, where are we going?" JT asked.

"C'mon, I'll show you," Cale said, leaping back on his board and continuing south toward the edge of town.

★   ★   ★

Half an hour later, Cale and JT reached a dusty turnoff where they were forced to step off their boards. Cale took the opportunity to get the water jug from his bag and take a long gulp. He also pulled out the printout of the map and jammed it into the front pocket of his jeans. He handed the jug to JT, who'd been ogling it since Cale had pulled it out. JT sucked back a swig.

"Where to?" JT asked, handing the bottle back to Cale.

"Over there," Cale said, pointing into the shimmering distance.

"Dude, you were going to do this alone?" JT said.

"Why not?" Cale asked.

"Because you might have gotten lost," JT said.

"We still could get lost," Cale said. "That's part of this test."

"What test?" JT asked.

"I figure this whole Empire thing is all about my dad *testing* me," Cale said.

"Really?" JT asked. "Sounds pretty stupid, if you ask me. Why the heck would he be sending you into crazy dangerous places?"

Cale thought for a moment. "'Cause he was tough enough to find and skate these places when he was our age, I guess."

"That's gnarly, man," JT said with a shrug. Then he smiled as he pulled an ancient cellphone from his pocket. "Well, if we do get lost, we've got this."

"Where'd you get that?" Cale asked.

"It's my mom's old one. She said I could have it for emergencies," JT said proudly.

"Does it work?" Cale asked.

"Yup," JT said, flipping it open like a pro. "It even takes pictures."

Cale looked way into the distance, where he could see the slash of the nameless dirt road. Everything looked much farther then he'd pictured it would be.

"Stay tough," Cale muttered, as he took his first step down the unnamed road.

★   ★   ★

It took them only twenty minutes to reach the end of the dirt road, where it ended unceremoniously at a small barricade. The soft dry wind rustled over piles of trash. A few motivated dumpers had even hauled ovens and washing machines into this part of the badlands.

"Which way from here?" JT asked.

Cale pulled the map from his jeans and shielded it with his hand so he could read it properly.

"That way," Cale said, holding his arm out diagonally into a particularly barren section of land. "Not too much longer."

But the badlands were far more hostile than Cale or even JT had imagined. Each step through the sand became more and more tiring, and the sun bore down on their backs with a fierce intensity.

They didn't say much, instead communicating with a series of grunts and "heys" when either one of them saw something interesting. "Interesting" things included prairie dogs, the odd milk snake, and a few old rusted tire rims.

After almost half an hour of walking, JT said what was on both of their minds. "You sure we're going the right way?"

Without markers or a road or anything besides the foothills that rose way in the distance, there was nothing of any significance that let them know they were on — or off — track.

"Yes," Cale said with certainty. "This is the way." He stopped and pointed straight ahead.

JT turned back and watched the wind make their most recent footsteps almost disappear. "Where would you say we came from?" JT asked, testing Cale.

"Right there," Cale said.

"Oh, man," JT said. "I would have said we came from there." He pointed in almost a completely different direction.

"What?" Cale said. "No way. Not possible." He spun on his feet, as his heart began beating faster and his ears began to ring. Everything around them looked the same. Sand and desert plants — that was it. No landmarks. Even the foothills seemed to surround them.

"We need to find shade," JT said. "Then we can think."

Cale wavered and lurched in the heat.

"There!" JT said. "Right up ahead. There's something."

JT jumped into the lead as Cale trudged behind.

JT was right. Five minutes later they approached the mystery object — an old, rusted flatbed trailer, still on its wheels.

They both ducked under the flatbed trailer into the relative coolness of the shade. Cale opened his bag and passed the jug of water to JT, who drank long from it, then passed it back to Cale. Cale lifted it up and looked at the fluid level — there was still half left — and although the water was warm, it felt good going down his parched throat. Cale reached into his bag and grabbed a granola bar, tossing it to JT.

"Lunch break," he said, forcing a smile.

JT opened the package with his teeth and spat the wrapper on the ground.

"Your phone!" Cale exclaimed. "I forgot about your phone."

JT pulled it from his pocket as he scarfed down the last of the snack.

"Shoot," JT said, his cheek full of melted granola. "No signal."

* * *

An hour later, the boys were still sitting in the shade, watching a long line of cloud pushing across the sky. It eventually reached the white blast of the sun and slowly began dulling the harshness of the day.

"Now's the time to make our move," Cale said, peering out into the distance in every direction, trying to get his bearings. The brownish red dirt of the distant foothills seemed to surround them. Though now, without the blast of the sun, the details of the world were easier to see.

Cale took a breath and ducked back under the rusted trailer. Sitting on the soft sand, he zipped up his backpack then reached into his sweat-soaked shirt and pulled out the charm that Angie had given him.

"What's that?" JT asked.

"It's, uh, it's just a good-luck thing Angie gave me," Cale said, lifting it up and squinting at the etching in the medal. For the first time he truly looked at the picture of St. Christopher, who was holding a staff in one hand and what appeared to be a boy on his shoulders. "It's for safe travels. Or something like that." A bead of sweat from Cale's forehead dripped onto the medallion, and he quickly wiped it away with his T-shirt.

JT jerked with a lazy laugh. "Safe travels. You plan on going somewhere? Besides here?"

At that moment, Cale turned his head and noticed something in the near distance.

"I said, you plan on going somewhere?" JT repeated.

"Yeah, I'm going there," he said, pointing. "The Desert Mirage!"

JT followed behind Cale as they left the shadow of the flatbed and began to walk toward a cluster of what looked like small single-storey houses. They hadn't noticed this little settlement before because it was the same colour as the surrounding foothills, which camouflaged it in the heat of the day.

Halfway to these earth-toned bungalows, a pang of worry leapt into Cale's chest. For a moment he thought that they might actually be a desert mirage, rather than being the Desert Mirage. The sun was gone, but the world in front of them still shimmered with heat, which made the small houses look like something out of a dream. It wasn't until Cale touched one of the houses' stuccoed sides that he knew it wasn't part of his imagination. He placed his palm on the shade side of one of the houses and felt a momentary wave of relief wash through him. JT pointed at a dusty old sign that lay flat on the ground and confirmed they were in the right place.

"The Desert Mirage," JT said as he read the sign. "We made it."

CHAPTER 12
THE ABANDONED WORLD

Cale and JT walked along the side of one of the crumbling buildings, where, in the afternoon glow, they followed a rocky path. Cale imagined that they were in some bombed-out war zone where enemies lurked in every shadow. As they silently passed the faded yellow wall of the first building, the trail gave way to a sort of courtyard surrounded by old pastel-coloured bungalows that clearly hadn't been lived in for a long time. The windows were either boarded up or just black holes leading into the shadows within. Doors with peeling paint had been ripped from hinges, and a sort of juvenile graffiti had been thrown up on some of the walls.

"What exactly are we looking for?" JT asked.

"I'm not sure," Cale said. "But I know there's gotta be something around here worth skating."

"The Orphans," JT said quietly, reading one particularly frightening piece of vandalism on the wall. Cale stared at the spot where the words were scrawled, taking note of a picture that accompanied them: a kind of a dagger, with trucks and wheels mounted to the blade, like the knife itself were a skateboard deck. The faded red paint had dried in a drippy kind of way that made it look like blood. It freaked Cale out, but at the same time it reassured him.

"They must be skaters," Cale said. "Why else would they draw trucks and wheels? We're getting close."

They crept toward the centre of the courtyard, where the crumbling remains of a brick and concrete fountain stood. It was rough and small — definitely not skateboard-worthy. They looked at each other and without saying a word agreed to continue on, deeper into this abandoned world.

They walked down a trail that ran beside a roofless pink bungalow. Cale stopped and peered inside it. Even in the dark he could see that holes had been punched and kicked into the white walls. There was more graffiti here, street art that followed a similar theme to the piece that JT had pointed out.

"Who do you think the Orphans are?" JT asked, pointing to two more spots where the words had been sprayed onto a piece of broken wooden fencing. Cale just shrugged.

They stole down the small footpath, which was strewn with shards of broken window glass; old, rusted beer cans; and dusty bricks. The trail curved a little and dropped down in a slant toward the shadows of a tall graffiti-tagged wall. Two words stood out on the wall, and Cale's lips moved as he read them: "NO HEROES."

That's when they heard a sound that froze them in their tracks.

★　　★　　★

It was a noise that was both haunting and familiar. A sound they'd both heard dozens of times, but in these unfamiliar and creepy surroundings it didn't excite them or relieve them — it scared them.

It was the unmistakable sound of skateboarding. They could hear skate wheels rolling aggressively across some sort of expanse in the near distance. Judging by the echoes of the wheels and the barking of the trucks grinding on concrete, Cale and JT knew, at the exact same moment, what it was these strangers were skating: an abandoned swimming pool.

The boys could also hear voices accompanying the sounds of skating, the unmistakable cheers of stoke from onlookers. This was the part that was scariest for JT and Cale — prompting them to look at each other, eyes wide, feet still frozen in their tracks. The fact was, these voices didn't just belong to strangers — they belonged to strange grown men.

Cale's stomach growled, and he immediately clutched it, worried that the sound would give them away. A smell of barbecued meat in the air had set his stomach off, and in that moment he realized how long it had been since he and JT had eaten anything besides melted granola bars.

"Gimme a boost," JT whispered, pointing to the wall with a mischievous look.

Cale silently hoisted JT up enough so that he could get a good look over. After a long moment, JT slid carefully down the wall and popped off Cale's shoulder, landing in the dirt like a cat.

JT smiled and flicked his head toward the wall, as if to say, *your turn.*

Cale swallowed and then stepped into JT's interlocked fingers. He pushed on JT's shoulder to get himself high enough to see just over the wall.

What he saw made his insides shrink. There had to be almost ten guys, all of them men, and most of them holding skateboards. They may have been skaters, but they looked more like a gang of bikers.

A few wore matching jean-jacket vests covered in patches. Those not in jean jackets were either in plaid shirts with the sleeves rolled up — showing tons of tattoos — or in no shirts at all. Most were standing on the concrete deck near the shallow end of an enormous, but empty, swimming pool. The kidney-shaped concrete hole was so thick with graffiti that it didn't resemble a normal pool in the slightest. Everything that would have normally been white or light blue was painted in dark reds, bright greens, and black. Cale's eyes landed on the deep end of the pool, where "The Orphans" was painted in large, rich red letters.

Cale became lost in the scene, watching one of the guys slash around the deep end with a frontside grind as the rest of the guys cheered him on. For a moment Cale forgot where he was, like he was in someone else's head or watching the entire spectacle on TV. He could feel JT under him, beginning to shake under Cale's weight, so he pulled himself up a little more on the wall's ledge to ease the strain. His eyes then darted to a row of Jeeps, pickup trucks, and cars parked off to one side of the pool, beyond a small fence with a broken gate.

Another car rolled into the lot, blaring punk rock. Two more skaters and their mongrel dog jumped out of the car. They left the music running.

Cale ducked down, afraid he might be seen; JT took this as a cue to slowly lower Cale from his perch. Cale jumped the last few feet himself, landing in the shadow at the foot of the wall.

"That pool is amazing, huh?" JT said.

It never occurred to Cale that they would actually try to skate this spot. He wanted nothing to do with that gnarly crew down there.

"Dude, let's get out of here. Let's go back," Cale whispered.

"What?" JT said. "No way! You said it yourself — it's a test. You'll fail the test if you don't skate that pool!"

Cale thought about what JT was saying, and though it shook him inside, he suspected JT was right.

"Okay, but we'll wait till they leave. Then we'll skate," Cale insisted.

And that's when someone grabbed their shoulders from behind.

"Who the hell are you guys?" a gruff voice asked.

JT tried to shake free of the hard grip, but it was no use; whoever it was had a serious grip. Cale's heart pounded in his ears as he cranked his head to look at their assailant — but instead he was shoved hard against the wall in front of them.

He crumpled onto the dusty ground.

"How did you get here?" the voice asked again.

Cale, climbing to his feet, was now able to look at the guy a little better. He was tall and broad, with a shaved head and the light stubble of a beard.

"Hey, Zeke!" the guy yelled. "Kill the music and get over here."

The music on the far side of the wall was silenced, and Cale and JT could hear the muffled voices of the men from behind the wall.

The first wave of guys rounded the corner with an urgency that made them look like they were ready for a fight. One of the guys held a piece of wood, making these guys look all the more menacing.

The guy in front of the pack, the one they called Zeke, stopped and stared at Cale and JT, who pressed their backs into the wall and prepared for the worst. Zeke was short but muscular, and his eyes were wild and amused.

"You guys lost or something?" the guy asked, stepping forward, but neither Cale nor JT answered. Instead, Cale slid the pack from one of his shoulders and reached into the rear pocket. He pulled out the old postcard and held it up, like some kind of peace offering.

Zeke slid it from Cale's hand slowly.

"Where did you get this?" he asked, flipping it over, then back, staring thoughtfully at the picture.

"My dad sent it to me," Cale said, gulping for air.

"Your dad?" said the guy who had first grabbed them.

"Yeah, his dad," JT barked.

Zeke squinted at Cale and cocked his head slightly to one side.

"Who's your dad?" Zeke asked.

"Lance Burns," Cale said.

Zeke closed his eyes and shook his head slowly, like he was trying to dislodge something from inside his head.

"That," Zeke said, "is a name I have not heard in a very, very long time."

CHAPTER 13
THE ORPHANS

Cale stood with his board notched into the coping at the shallow end of the pool. He had never skated a pool like this one, but he knew how to skate mini-ramps and quarter-pipes. The rounded corners might take some getting used to, but first he had to impress the Orphans, who had all stopped what they were doing to watch him.

"What are you waiting for, Cale?" JT whispered with a smile. "It's only a gang of gnarly dudes watching your every move."

Cale smiled and then dropped in, pumping down the bump from shallow to deep end and racing across the bottom of the pool. He climbed the farthest, deepest wall, rising as it reached vert, and scratched out a frontside grind on the well-worn coping. This simple trick yielded a chorus of cheers from the Orphans, who lined the deck.

Cale zipped back down the wall, rolling up into the shallow end. His face betrayed the surprise that even he felt.

"That was rad!" Cale said as he rolled up to JT. "And fast!"

JT dropped next, and he rolled into the deep end and expertly carved around its painted lip. He then attacked the right wall, locking into a fifty-fifty stall, before dropping back in. Another round of cheers came from the Orphans. It was clear they were impressed with these two kids.

Cale dropped in again and decided to try something else now that he was used to the contours. This time, he popped a frontside ollie when he reached the lip and piloted his board with a skill years beyond his age.

More cheers from the old dudes.

"Kind of dangerous for you guys to walk out in the middle of the desert," Zeke said. "Don'tcha think?"

Zeke was still holding the postcard like it was a fragile ancient relic that had just been pulled from an archeologist's dig site.

"Who else has seen this?" Zeke asked.

"Nobody. I mean, just me . . . and my mom," Cale said. He looked at his watch. It was almost 7:00 p.m. She might be starting to worry.

"Hold on a sec," Cale said to Zeke. "I'll be right back."

He ducked away from Zeke and found JT about to drop in for another run.

"JT, can I try your phone again?" Cale asked. JT handed it to Cale, flipping it open.

"The only place you are going to get service," one of the Orphans called out, "is up there." He pointed to an old, crumbled diving tower covered in graffiti.

Moments later, Cale had climbed to the top. One signal bar appeared on the phone after a few moments. He immediately dialed his home number.

After a few rings, his mom picked up. "There you are," she said. "I was beginning to worry."

"Nothing to worry about, Mom, but I might be kind of late tonight," he said.

"How late are we talking?" his mom asked.

"I dunno, maybe another hour or so, but don't worry, I'm with some guys who used to know Dad," Cale said, before realizing that this might not have been the wisest thing for him to say.

"What?" Cale's mom said. "What are you talking about, Cale?"

"Nothing. I mean, I'm fine, Mom. I'm safe," Cale said. "I really need you to trust me here."

There was silence on the other end. It lasted so long that Cale pulled the phone from his ear to check and see if it had lost its signal.

"Mom?"

"I'm still here, Cale," she huffed. "No later than nine. I'm being generous here."

Cale sighed loudly and dropped his head. He hung up the phone, and as he looked down on the pool and the guys, he realized just how crazy this particular adventure had been.

Peering over the edge of the old diving tower, he looked at the scene below. The Orphans, their dogs, the painted pool — it looked so surreal to him. He lifted the old phone up and snapped a wide picture of the Orphans' pool. He had to prove to his father that they'd actually made it there and lived to tell about it. In his own mind, he figured he'd passed another test.

When he came down the ladder Zeke was standing there, still holding the postcard.

"Come with me," Zeke said, motioning with his head toward a graffiti-covered picnic table. "You hungry?"

"Yeah! I mean, yes, sir. All we had to eat today was some melted granola bars."

"Hey, Vin! Get these kid some burgers," Zeke snapped to a shirtless tattooed guy manning the barbeque. "Don't ever call me 'sir.' I'm not your old man."

"Oh, okay, sorry," Cale said, as a big burger wrapped in a bun was slapped down on a paper plate in front of him. He ripped into a big bite. He was so hungry he barely remembered how to chew.

"I want to talk about your dad," Zeke said. "What do you know about him? Are you two close?"

Cale just shrugged. "Not really. I haven't even met him — yet," he said through a mouthful of burger.

"So then why is he sending you things like this?" Zeke asked, sliding the postcard on the table toward Cale. "If you've never met him."

Cale swallowed. "It's a game."

"A game. What kind of game?" Zeke asked.

"Like a test. He wants me to find all of the old places he used to skate," Cale said. "He calls those spots the Empire."

Zeke stared at Cale for a long time. "A game. And how's the *game* goin' so far?"

Cale wiped his hands on his jeans after his final bite. "Well, we've found the first two places: the Tombstones, which was on a kind of hidden map he gave me, and we've found, well, here. This place. The clue was that postcard."

"Nothing else?" Zeke asked.

"Not yet. But once I tell him about this place, he'll hopefully let me know about the next one," Cale said, realizing he may have said too much.

Zeke turned his head sideways. "You plan on telling anyone else about this place?"

Cale's right knee began to jerk in a nervous spasm, and all of a sudden he felt sick to his stomach. "This place? You mean here? Well, no. No way."

Zeke looked at Cale for a long time before he spoke again.

"You know, I knew your dad," Zeke said. "He was the guy we looked up to when we were younger. He was the best skater around."

"Was he . . . um . . . ?" Cale stammered as he reached for the right question. "What was he like, I mean, off his board?"

Zeke gazed off into the near distance, in a trance. After what felt like a full minute, he spoke. "We called him Sir Lancelot. Sounds lame, but in many ways he was like a knight. Even though he was a tough-nut skateboarder he was always polite. He always said 'yes, sir' and 'no, ma'am' and all that. But underneath that polite guy there was this *fire*," Zeke said.

"A fire?" Cale echoed.

"Yeah, a real drive. He was the one who found all of these places," Zeke said, gesturing to the paint-splattered pool. "We called him Sir Lancelot because he was always on some kind of quest. Always searching for something. Seems to be a theme with you guys."

"Yeah, sure, I guess," Cale said. "What do you think he was searching for? I mean, besides skate spots?"

"Beats me. Maybe he just wanted to get outta town. But here's the problem with Lance and a life spent searching. Pretty soon the search becomes the destination. You know what I mean?

Cale didn't really, but he nodded anyway. He rolled the thought into his mind, saving it for a moment when he could actually think about what it meant.

"I don't mean to upset you — I mean he is your dad and everything. But his whole searching trip leaves a lot of upset people in its wake. I mean, I thought we were pals, then he just *left*. Never came back. Never even sent me one of these," Zeke said, tapping the postcard. "And we were thick as thieves."

"My mom said kinda the same thing," Cale said. "That he just left us. No warning."

"You gotta be careful with him, Cale," Zeke said. "Even if he is your dad."

Cale dug into the ground with his shoes and stared blankly at the graffiti-topped table.

"I know how you feel, man. I never knew my dad — or my mom, really. I don't think your dad did either. That's how we came up with the name 'the Orphans' for our crew," Zeke said. "All of us knew how it felt to be let down."

"What does 'NO HEROES' mean?" Cale asked.

"It means we don't need anybody. Only thing that matters is me, myself," Zeke said proudly. "You should keep that in mind on your . . ." Zeke laughed to himself, "*quest.*"

★   ★   ★

The middle of the following week, Ryan and Skylar returned from skate camp, and with them came a bunch of amazing stories. From seeing pros at skate demos, to having insane food fights, to meeting amazing skaters from across the country — there seemed to be no end to the tales they told.

But JT and Cale never told the guys about their trip into the badlands. In a way it was scary to talk about, or even think about, how close to disaster they had been.

The only person Cale did tell was his dad. He wrote the entire tale in an email. It felt good to spill the story to someone, and at two full pages it was the longest thing he'd ever written. He tried his best to get all the details correct. Right down to the number of snakes they saw, how scared he had been, as well as the number of tricks he was able to pull off in the bowl. Along with the email, Cale had sent the photo he had taken with JT's cellphone. It wasn't the clearest or best shot ever, but it did show proof that Cale had found the second location in the Empire. Now his dad would know that the Desert Mirage was now the Orphans' bowl. Or maybe his dad already knew that. Cale had no idea. He still hadn't heard a peep back, and it had been almost four days.

The only part of the story he left out was the stuff that Zeke had said. He didn't tell that to anyone.

That night when Cale went to sleep, two words rolled around in his head over and over: NO HEROES.

CHAPTER 14
THE SINKHOLE

A few days later, when Cale was just about to head out and skate, the doorbell rang. Cale got to the door first and opened it to see a man dressed in the blue-and-white uniform of a parcel delivery service. The man smiled as he held out two different packages.

"I got something for a Margot Finch and something for a Cale Finch. I'm guessing you're not Margot? Am I right?" He laughed.

Cale smiled. "I'm Cale. My mom is Margot."

"I need an adult to sign for them," the man said. "Unless you're the man of the house!" He laughed again at his own joke.

"Mom!" Cale called out. "She'll be down in a second."

He stared at the packages. The addresses and the names on both packages looked as if the same hand had written them. Cale knew the penmanship: the same person who had written Cale's name and address on the postcard.

A few moments later Cale's mom bounced down from upstairs, putting on her earrings.

"Sign here, ma'am," the man said, holding out a small digital terminal. "I was just laughing with your boy here, asking if he was the man of the house." He laughed again.

Cale's mom signed, then grabbed both parcels. "He is indeed the man of the house," she said, smiling before closing the door.

She handed Cale the large envelope with his name on it and tucked the small one into her purse.

"I'm heading into the city for a meeting but I'll be home for lunch at our regular time. Will that work?" she asked.

"I dunno, I might just eat with the guys," he said.

Cale thought about asking her to open her envelope right then and there but decided against it. His mind shifted gears — all he wanted to do was tear into the package he'd been sent.

He raced into town, ollieing everything in his path, excited to meet up with the guys, but when he arrived to the Plaza, he was the only one there.

He couldn't wait any longer. He sat on a bench

in the shade and delicately opened one end of the envelope. He dusted off the bench and then carefully poured the contents out. First, a small black and white picture dropped out, then a larger colour picture, then a large but very thin piece of folded tracing paper.

Cale picked up the black and white photo and studied it. It was hard to tell what it was at first, or from what angle it had been taken. It kind of looked like a big porcelain sink in a fancy restroom, but somehow different. He set it down on the bench. Then he gently picked up the colour picture, holding it by the edges. He had seen this shot before in a pile of old pictures of his father. Now, he scanned every inch of the picture carefully, looking for a clue.

It was a shot of his dad carving a huge backside turn, high on the steep face of the big concrete bowl. The turn was well above a big grate, covering a sewer tube that was almost large enough for a person to stand up in. Above the grate, someone had messily spray painted the words "thE SiNkHOLE" in bright green.

Next he moved on to the folded tracing paper. He opened it up carefully, afraid to rip the fragile, yellowed paper, and out fell a small white three-by-five index card. On it, written in his father's hand, were the words: "Enjoy the Ride — with Edwin!"

Cale studied the tracing paper and tried to make out what was on it, but the writing was so faded it was very hard to read. It almost didn't look like a map at all, but more like some kind of alien galaxy, drawn in light blue pencil. A series of thin lines spread out like spokes from one central, circular hub. Cale was pretty sure the lines were roads. However, very long numbers, which Cale had never seen, were written on some of the blue lines, making his road-map theory seem less likely. Cale held it up to the light hoping something would become clearer, but it was nearly impossible for him to make sense of it.

He heard the thunder of skate wheels on the Plaza floor, and a few seconds later, JT appeared, eating a bag of chips.

"Hey, bro," JT said. When he noticed what Cale was doing, his eyes popped open. "Is that what I think it is?"

"I don't know what it is," Cale sighed. "I mean, I know it's the third spot in the Empire but I have no idea how we're gonna find it."

Skylar and Josh rolled up.

"Why is it on that kind of paper?" JT asked.

"Tracing paper," Josh said. "My dad uses that stuff all the time on his drafting table."

"What for?" Skylar asked.

"To trace with, bonehead," Josh said. "This piece looks pretty old. So, is this the next clue?"

"I guess so," Cale said. "But we can't really make any sense of it. Or this."

Cale handed Josh the black and white picture of the basin.

Josh turned his head to the side and his eyes lit up.

"Holy cow!" he said. "You know what this is?" He passed the picture to JT.

"No idea," JT said. "A shadow or something? I don't know, man."

Josh pointed it out to Cale. He was right, there was an odd shadow over the basin, and Cale squinted to make it out.

"Dude," Josh said. "That's the shadow of a helicopter. This shot was taken from that helicopter." He grabbed the colour shot of Cale's dad.

"This," Josh said, holding up the black and white shot, "is an aerial view of this." He held up the colour shot.

"It's a giant bowl," Cale said, realizing the scale of what they were looking at. It was a bowl that was almost ten times larger than the Orphans' empty pool.

"But where is it?" Skylar said, leaning in. "I mean, is it still around?" Skylar grabbed the colour shot of Cale's dad. "I mean, no offence, but this picture has gotta be, like, twenty years old. Look — his board doesn't even have a nose."

More wheels roared through the Plaza, and when the guys turned they were shocked to see Toby. It had been two weeks, and by the way he was skating it looked like his ankle had healed up nicely. He rolled with a confidence that Skylar, JT, and Josh had never seen. He even had a unique style that made his pushes seem effortless. From behind him, Ryan rolled into sight, catching up to Toby. Cale's heart went into his throat. What was Ryan going to do? Start making fun of him behind his back? Push him off his board into one of the planters?

Toby, rolling toward the guys with this new vibe of self-confidence, bent low and cracked a perfect kickflip — as good as one that JT or Cale or any of the guys could do. He landed it smoothly and rolled to a stop right by the stunned crew.

"Ankle's better," Toby said, lifting his foot and rolling it around.

"Dudes, I followed this guy," Ryan said, pointing at Toby, "all the way from the top of Main Street. And he was amazing!"

Toby tapped his board with his feet and looked at the guys with pride.

"He ollied literally everything in his path," Ryan said. "It was sick."

Toby looked at Cale. "Well, I have a good teacher," he said. "Another week of healing, and I'm going to try those stairs again."

★   ★   ★

Two days later, Cale sat the local skateboard shop, frustrated. All of the Plaza skating had worn flat spots in his wheels and he needed new ones. Darius, the guy who ran the shop, knew Cale didn't have a lot of money, so he gave him used product at a deep discount, often for nothing. But that's not what made him feel defeated. It was the way Darius had reacted to Cale's topic of conversation: the Sinkhole.

The tracing paper and the photos of the spot lay on the glass display case of the skate shop. After he finished with the wheels, Darius looked at the colour photo one more time.

"Dude. Like I said, I think it's just a legend. Ancient history. It would be cool if was a real spot around here. But it ain't," Darius said. "Rumour is it was bulldozed or somethin'."

Cale collected the photos and the map, tucking them back into his bag.

"If you find it though, little man, you come tell me!" Darius said.

The skate shop was one of the many places Cale had gone to, looking for info. He showed the tracing-paper map to Ryan's dad, who was a real estate agent and knew more about Drayton than anyone, but he was no help. He took the map to the parks department in Drayton and came up empty-handed there too. Cale was beginning to believe that the Sinkhole was just a legend. But that didn't explain the pictures. Cale still had faith.

He thought back to the first two packages his father had sent. As he rolled through town later that afternoon, he thought of the first map, which was clear as day once he had found the Tombstones. He thought of the postcard, which was an actual photo of the spot — the first two clues to the first two spots contained all the information he'd needed to find them. Now all Cale had were puzzle pieces that didn't fit together or point him in any direction.

He was stumped. More than anything, he was worried about what his dad would think if he failed.

"Enjoy *what* ride?" Cale said to himself as he started to gain speed down a small hill.

"And who's Edwin?" Cale thought as he took a breath and felt the warm summer breeze tousle his hair. He felt very attached to that moment, and as he reached full speed he thought about how his summer had gone thus far. He'd had adventures that had taken him to places he'd never thought he'd go, and he'd mentored Toby and turned him into a better skater. As Cale's speed started to decline and the road levelled out he said to himself. "I am 'enjoying the ride.'"

Then it dawned on him.

"Enjoy the Ride — with Edwin!" he said again. "Where do I know that from?"

He opened his backpack and looked at the white index card. "Enjoy the Ride," he said. "Capital *E*. Capital *R*."

Cale knew exactly where he'd seen those words written in that style. He jumped back on his board and headed to Drayton's north end.

CHAPTER 15
OLDE DRAYTON

Cale stood in front of the old used-car dealership, which was nothing more than a large, double-wide trailer and a parking lot with a few hundred cars in it. Coloured flags ringed the property, flapping lazily in the hot breeze. On top of the trailer was a sign that said "ED ROGERS" in faded yellow, and hung from a line of flagging at the front of the lot was an ancient sign with the words "Enjoy the Ride — with Edwin!"

The place looked closed, maybe even forever. A few cars had a thick layer of desert dust on them. Someone had drawn a peace symbol and written "Wash Me" on the hood of a beige convertible.

Cale walked to the front door of the trailer and was about to knock when he noticed that the door was partially open. He knocked anyway, and the door slowly creaked open.

Cale heard a grumbling and a rustling of paper.

"I'll be right there," said a deep voice coming from the back.

Cale stood in the afternoon haze of the trailer. It was dark, and there were a few flies buzzing around the window.

The fluorescent lights overhead clicked and a few flickered on. Cale scanned around the wood-panelled room and saw a high counter in front of a few desks piled high with paper and files. Old, yellowed car posters clung to the wall next to a calendar from 1988.

"I get the feeling you're not looking for a car," said a small, hunched man who shuffled his way around the counter. "You looking for a job? Because my son's not here, and he's the guy to talk to if you want a job."

"No, I don't want a job, I actually . . ." It dawned on Cale that he really didn't have any idea why he was there. He unzipped his backpack and pulled out the tracing paper. "Do you have any idea what this is?" Cale asked.

The man held the tracing paper in a shaky hand and opened it up. He whistled to himself, lifted his reading glasses up, and held them in front of his face.

"Hmm," the man said. "Can't say I do."

Cale took out the index card and the two

photos and placed them on the counter. He tapped the index card.

"This is what brought me here," Cale said. "But I get the feeling I've come to the wrong place."

"Enjoy the Ride," the man said. "Yup, that's my slogan. Though my new slogan should be 'Enjoy the Recession.'" He laughed, handing the tracing paper back to Cale. But he stopped laughing abruptly when he saw the colour photo of Cale's dad on the counter.

"Say, I remember that kid. He used to work for me. Lance somebody-or-other."

"He did?"

"Yeah, shuttling cars around the lot," he said. "Very dependable guy."

"Really?" Cale said, amazed. *Dependable*?

"I remember it like it was yesterday. He walked in off the street and said, 'There's a yellow '67 Mustang on the lot that's getting dusty. That's no way to treat a car that cool.' He told me he used to work at a car wash, knew everything there was to know about keeping cars in showroom condition. I hired him on the spot. Three bucks an hour. I'm glad I did because, as I found out later, that kid had it tough."

"What do you mean, *tough*?" Cale asked

"Dad long gone, mom with troubles of her own.

He was living with an aunt who didn't have much use for him. Practically an orphan." The man said this with his vacant eyes staring straight ahead out the dusty window.

"An orphan . . ." Cale echoed.

The man sighed. "He was a nice kid. But he always seemed to be, I dunno, looking past you, like he was looking for the next thing . . . for something else. Restless, y'know?"

Cale's insides bunched up as a fly buzzed around the humming overhead light, making him dizzy.

"Then one day he just up and left Drayton. Stopped by here for one last look at the Mustang and that was it. Wanted to go and find his dad, he did. He held some crazy notion that he'd gone to California. Found out later that he'd left a pregnant girlfriend behind. The girlfriend was the one that painted that mural."

Cale turned dizzily toward the door and couldn't believe his eyes. On the wall was a painting: a fancy sort of map of "Olde Drayton," the way the town must have looked a hundred years ago. Scenes from the distant past painted with striking realism surrounded the simple but still beautiful map. There were miners digging in the hills, horse-drawn buggies and old cars on Main Street, a man sitting cross-legged with a gun on his lap.

"He used to bring her around to look at the cars. Joke about buying the Mustang for her. She was sweet on him, that was easy to see. And he was a different kind of kid when she came around. A little less jumpy-like."

Cale walked slowly toward the painting, immediately recognizing the touch of his mother's brush. He placed a hand on the painting, realizing that this was the reason he had come. He took a step back and held the tracing paper up to the mural. A large image of a wagon wheel anchoring the left bottom corner jumped out at him, and when he placed the tracing paper over the spokes of the wheel, it fit perfectly.

"Well, I'll be . . ." said the man from over Cale's shoulder.

Cale smoothed the tracing paper out and could feel small depressions that had been carved into the painting once it had dried. Cale pulled the sheet off, and could see that these ridges had been done with the point of a knife, and looked more like the work of his father than his mother.

"Do you have a pencil?" Cale asked. The man scooted around the counter and grabbed a pencil from one of the desks. He brought it to Cale.

Cale very carefully rubbed the pencil back and forth across the tracing paper, and after a moment or so, an image began to form. Another minute of pencil rubbing and Cale was done. He pulled the tracing paper from the wall and carefully walked it under a buzzing fluorescent light. It was a map. A main road gave way to a series of smaller roads. At the top of these roads was what appeared to be the massive basin. The Sinkhole. Cale walked back to the map on the wall and got his bearings.

The map on the tracing paper was a map of the industrial park. Definitely not something that should have been on a map of "Olde Drayton."

"Incredible," he said.

"You're telling me," the old man said. "There hasn't been this much excitement here in years."

"My mom painted that," Cale said proudly. "Not sure she ever knew it would become a clue."

"So the guy in this picture . . . ?" the man asked.

"Is my dad," Cale said.

CHAPTER 16
INTO THE TUNNEL

The very next day, the Seven Stair Crew plus Toby found themselves on the number ten bus. Cale figured the bus was the best way to get them out to the industrial park that was nestled below the hills on the outskirts of Drayton.

"How much farther is this place, man?" Skylar said as the bus lurched over yet another bump in the road. "It feels like we've been on this stupid bus for an hour."

Cale wasn't listening to Skylar's complaints and neither were the rest of the guys — they were all poring over the pencil-rubbed map, trying to figure it out.

Cale was looking out of the bus windows at the small foothills that didn't appear big at all. They resembled rocky sand dunes from this distance, but he knew that up close they were really massive.

"This is our stop," Cale said, standing up and pulling the yellow "stop requested" cord that ran the length of the bus.

"Service Road and Millman Industrial Park," a pre-recorded female voice announced.

The guys jumped off the bus and immediately onto their skateboards, heading in the direction of the low, grey factories and white warehouses of the industrial park.

It was almost four-thirty and some of the industrial park workers were leaving for home.

Cale led the crew to the tail end of the cul-de-sac at the end of the industrial park closest to the hills that towered above them. Cale looked left and right, looking for the overflow tunnel, but he couldn't see it anywhere. It was a dead end.

"Check along the sides. Spread out!" Ry called out. "I've got this side, okay?"

Cale dragged his foot a little to slow down and rolled to the opposite end, and the rest of the crew did the same, fanning out into different directions. A moment later, they heard Skylar call out.

"Cale! Check this out!"

The rest of the guys joined him by a hedge, the centre of which was blowing around like it was in front of a big fan. Cale went first and ducked under the prickly plants.

"Holy crow," he said. "This must be it."

"Did you hear that?" JT said, still on the other side of the bushes. "It sounded like thunder."

"No, it's just the sound of the wind, man," Cale said. "It echoes through this whole tunnel."

The tunnel was big enough for everyone (except Josh) to stand up in without having to crouch.

"How far does it go?" Skylar said.

"I dunno," Cale said as he secured his skateboard to the straps of his backpack and slung it over his shoulders.

Cale went first, followed by Toby, Josh, JT, Skylar, and Ry. Ry backed his way into the tunnel behind the rest of the crew.

"I've got a weird feeling about this," Ry said with a shaky voice, but nobody could hear him. They were almost fifty feet ahead of him, around a little curve, heading toward a little spot of light at the other end of the tunnel.

Two minutes into the tunnel, Cale stopped, realizing that he was way ahead of the rest of the guys. He paused and listened to the sound of the wind whooshing by and his friends' skate shoes echoing through the giant cylinder. In front of him the tunnel dipped down on a slant. He cautiously began to walk down the slant, using his hand on the rounded side of the full-pipe to steady himself.

"It gets kinda steep here, guys, so watch your step!" he called back.

At the bottom of the steep section, the tunnel opened into a large room, almost as big as the small gym at his school. On the far side of the room was a big slanted ramp with little bits of dried grass stuck to the sides. Cale didn't need his flashlight in the vaulted room because four or five small holes about the size of basketballs on the side of the wall near the ceiling let in big shafts of afternoon light. On the floor of the room were two huge holes, just about as wide as the tunnel they'd entered. The floor holes were covered with grates, like thick jail bars.

Cale got down on all fours and yelled into one of the holes with the deepest voice he could muster. "Hell-o!" he called, not really expecting an answer.

He straightened up and looked around some more. "Dad must have taken the same route in," Cale said to himself. "It's like I'm walking in his footsteps."

Cale could hear the rest of the guys coming down the slant, so he scrambled up the opposite side and continued farther down the next tunnel that opened up there. He could hear the rest of the guys marvelling at the chamber and calling for Cale to wait up.

Josh was the first of the guys to catch up to Cale, and when he did, they were less than a hundred paces away from the end of the tube. They could see the light spilling in from outside.

"Is that another grate?" Josh asked, squinting.

"Not sure," Cale said. "Let's find out."

"Hang on, guys." A voice pulsed from the darkness behind them. It could have been Toby, Skylar, or JT — it was hard to tell.

Cale and Josh didn't slow down one bit. They were almost at the end, and as they got closer and closer they went faster and faster.

"Man, it is a grate," Cale said. "It'd better open."

They were only steps away now, and they could see the massive rusted iron bars coming into focus. Sunlight poured through the grate, forcing Cale and Josh to squint as they busied themselves with trying to open the barrier. Cale pushed with all his might, but the cage-like door wouldn't open.

"Here, maybe this will work," Josh said, removing a big piece of wood that was jammed between the side of the tunnel and the edge of the grate.

The door began to swing open with a massive squeak, like the gate to an old cemetery would sound if hadn't been oiled in years. Josh held the stick in his hands; it was heavy for its size and really smooth.

"This is driftwood," Josh said. "The kind of stuff you see on riverbanks and stuff. What's it doing here?"

"I dunno," Cale said. Uninterested in the wood, he turned to the rest of the crew and yelled back through the tunnel, "C'mon, guys!"

"Anyway," Josh continued, "it looks like someone wedged it in there on purpose." He tossed the stick on the ground and helped Cale push the grate the rest of the way open.

"Watch it!" Cale said as he pushed the gate as far open as he could, almost falling over the edge. It was a good thing he didn't because the pipe dropped off to a near-vertical drop to the bottom. JT, Toby, and Skylar had caught up now, and it was JT who saw the enormity of the bowl first.

"Holy crap," JT said, sticking his head out of the tunnel and taking full stock of what was before them.

Cale hadn't been too far off when he'd mistaken the aerial photograph for a fancy porcelain basin, because that's exactly what it looked like. He elbowed for position as he scanned the bowl. It was at least one hundred feet lengthwise and almost forty-five feet wide. It felt like a coliseum. Directly across from them was a big channel about thirty feet long that stretched toward the mountains in the background. It was shaped like a mellow half-pipe about five feet high and it spilled over two big rolling hips into the main part of the bowl.

JT lowered himself down from the tunnel and slid effortlessly on the soles of his shoes to the bottom of the basin.

"This is insane!" he yelled back up to the guys.

He looked so tiny standing in the flat-bottom of the basin, and his voice echoed off the sides a few times into the dry air.

One by one they lowered themselves down into the bowl, marvelling at its enormity and the smoothness of the concrete. Cale turned his head a full three-sixty, taking in every curve and twist of the Sinkhole. He looked up directly above the tunnel that had led them in and saw the familiar green graffiti he'd seen in the shot with his dad carving over the whole grate. It had faded a lot, but it was still visible. "The Sinkhole," it read.

"I can't believe your dad used to skate here," Toby said, climbing up the far wall toward the mellow half-pipe that acted as a roll-in to the massive bowl.

The rest of the guys followed JT up to the natural starting point of the Sinkhole. Cale climbed up even higher out of the half-pipe and onto the reddish desert dirt. He could see the town of Drayton shimmering in the heat of the day like a mirage. He spun around and saw the arid land behind him, cracked and rising like a great sandy wall. Behind the ridge of low mountains Cale could see dark sheets of cloud cover, way off in the distance, which were slowly folding in upon themselves like smoke from a brush fire.

"Someone has been here recently," Ry said breathlessly. He held up a shiny beer can as evidence.

JT started to pump back and forth in the little half-pipe, kicking turns back and forth.

"Okay, who's goin' first?" he asked. It was a practical question, but the whole crew was in such awe of the place they had forgotten the reason they wanted to find it.

"Cale should," said Josh. "It's his quest, after all."

Cale did not hesitate. Lowering himself down into the half-pipe and dropping his backpack to the ground, he unlatched his board from the straps and tossed his bag up to Toby.

Cale gave one push toward the steep shoulder that dropped from the half-pipe and spilled into the giant bowl. He teetered on the edge for a split second and then, with increasing speed, he disappeared, plunging down into the massive basin of the Sinkhole.

Cale absorbed the transition and pumped for speed down the roll-in. The concrete was so smooth under his wheels that they shrieked with a sound he'd never heard before. He approached the massive wall directly opposite and arced a turn high into the vert, right beside the tunnel that had led them in. He stalled for an instant before zipping back down the transition and across the almost non-existent flat-bottom of the basin. Before he knew it, he was almost at the top of the roll, which at this speed, served as a perfect launch ramp for him. He bent his knees and smacked an ollie at the top of the incline and floated a perfect Indy grab at least three feet off the ground, landing perfectly beside his friends.

"Yeah!" they shouted, realizing that the basin would be perfect not only for carving big turns but also for popping big airs and floating huge ollies. What also became clear was that the hips that poured into the basin could be aired over, transfer-style, into the small half-pipe where they all stood.

Without a word, JT dropped from sight down the roll-in and into the stadium-sized bowl. He carved a massive, stylish turn around the eastern side and floated up over the hip with a big head-high ollie. As he dropped into the half-pipe, he popped a backside disaster on the far wall and then stepped off his board, almost falling down on the transition.

He caught his balance and grabbed his board,

jogging down the side of one of the walls to where everyone was standing.

"That was sick, bro!" Skylar said, slapping him a high-five.

JT was out of breath with excitement, "And I hardly even hit my tail!" he said, exhaling. "It's like this place was *meant* for skating. It's perfect!"

Ryan went next, doing some kick turns and carving the wide part of the bowl. Even though he didn't pop any ollies or catch any air, he had a great run that seemed to last almost five full minutes. He calmly rode up the roll-in with a huge grin on his face.

"This place is the best — it's like you never run out of speed!"

Skylar surprised everyone by pushing from the deepest recess of the half-pipe and hitting the hip on his way in to the bowl. He floated a perfect frontside flip and took the first drop riding fakie, which was super insane, but he landed it, and rolled up the opposite wall backwards.

The crew cheered as he sped back down toward the roll-in and spun a nollie three-flip at least four feet off the ground. It spun out of control and Skylar was unable to land it, but he was still sporting a grin ear to ear.

"Good thing I'll have the rest of the summer to perfect that one!" he said.

Josh followed Skylar's lead and popped a big frontside one-eighty ollie over the hip and rode down the transition backwards. He rolled up the far side of the wall like Skylar had, but then Josh did something that no one else had even thought of: He stalled his tail where the wall met with the tunnel. He paused for a second, looked over his shoulder into the blackness of the tunnel and then dropped back down into the bowl, shooting across the bottom of the basin and up the roll-in. He popped an ollie and then slapped high-fives with the rest of the crew.

All eyes drifted over to Toby.

"Dude, it's your turn," Cale said. He looked at the rest of the guys. "Right, guys?"

"For sure, Toby," said JT. "It's all you."

"You can do it, man," said Josh.

Ryan and Skylar also chimed in with support. Toby slowly set his board down, stood on it, and rolled toward the lip.

Cale could see the fire in Toby's eyes return as Toby gave a big push and disappeared down into the bowl. The rest of the guys ran to the edge to make sure he was okay, and sure enough he was. He rocketed across the flat-bottom, up the far wall where he did a textbook kick turn, and returned toward them.

The crew cheered, but for some reason, Toby wasn't smiling. Instead, he rolled up toward the guys with a weird look in his eye.

"I think something is coming," he said.

CHAPTER 17
DISTANT RUMBLING

The crew stood on the far side of the bowl at the bottom of the smooth half-pipe-like ditch and stared at the foothills behind them. They didn't make a sound; they just stood there listening and watching — waiting for something to happen. In the distance there was the slight rumble of thunder from a storm somewhere far away. It made every one of them a little bit more anxious.

A loud shudder of thunder echoed around the rim of the bowl as a few big raindrops fell from the still-sunny sky.

The ground under everyone's feet began to rumble, and the little stones and sand began to jump around like heated popcorn.

What the heck was going on?

"Is it an e-e-earthquake?" asked JT.

Out of nowhere a small trickle of water ran into

the ditch. It rolled past their feet, and made its way into the larger bowl of the Sinkhole.

"Get up on the sides! Get up, get up!" Toby screamed to everybody as he scrambled up the wall of the little half-pipe. Toby swung his arm around and pointed up toward the hills.

"It's a flash flood. From the mountains. I've read about these things. We've got to get out of here!"

Everybody tried to scramble up the banks above and onto the flat, dry, reddish earth of the desert, but JT and Josh stopped dead in their tracks as they turned and looked toward the hills. At first it looked to them like a sand slide or mini-rock avalanche coming down a crease in the hills. But the rocks and sand stopped sliding after a few seconds and the ground stopped rumbling.

"Get out of there now!" Toby yelled to JT and Josh. "I mean it! You've all got to get out now!"

Then Cale saw it. Out of nowhere, a wall of dirty water almost as big as a surf wave was charging around the corner of the low hills and directly toward them. It took less than two seconds for it to reach them as it crashed into the little half-pipe spillway, taking JT and Josh and Cale's backpack with it. The great wave lashed like a tongue, overflowing the sides of the ditch and knocking Toby onto his butt, almost sucking him down into the turbulent mud-coloured river.

Cale ran along the edge of the bowl. Everybody did the same, screaming loudly after JT and Josh. As Cale peered over the steep edge of the basin he could see no signs of anyone. All he could see was the water rising in the bowl, like in a great big toilet.

The two heads of JT and Josh looked awfully small as they popped to the surface of the swelling water that was continuing to rise and twist like a whirlpool. Skylar and Ryan had reached down and, by a stroke of luck, been able to grab Josh's arm, but it looked like the surge of the flood was about to pull them in too. Cale ran over, grabbed Ryan's back, and managed to help them pull Josh to the side. They eventually laid him down safely in the dirt, where he curled up coughing and wheezing.

The water was still rising and it was only a matter of moments before it was going to start to spill out of the Sinkhole and down the tunnel that had brought them all in. Cale pictured the central chamber and the two big grate-covered tunnels that shot down into the earth. Anyone who got sucked into the overflow tunnel was done for.

A little stream of overflowing water that rolled by Cale's feet was carrying a glistening skateboard, and he grabbed it by one wheel. It wasn't his, but he thought he would save whatever he could at this point.

"JT is still in there!" somebody yelled. "We've got to get JT!"

"There!" Skylar yelled, pointing at a little bobbing head near the centre of the Sinkhole. "He's right there!"

The water was still rising and beginning to splash into the overflow tunnel. Everyone watched in shock as JT spun around the outside of the basin like a matchstick flushed into a giant toilet. As Cale looked down, JT locked eyes with him.

"Guys!" Cale yelled. "We can use this!" He held up the skateboard he'd found by its front truck. Toby, Skylar, and Ryan dashed toward Cale.

"Lower me down the side, over the tunnel. I'll try to pass the skateboard to him," Toby said.

Cale and Skylar grabbed Toby's legs and lowered him down slowly.

It took a minute or so, but the water eventually forced JT in a direct line toward Toby, who held the skateboard as tightly as he could by the front truck.

The timing had to be perfect in order to get the board into JT's hand, or he'd go around the whirlpool again or get sucked into the overflow tunnel, a quarter of which was covered with the rising water.

Cale used his other arm to push Toby off the wall so he could stretch the board to JT as he passed. JT missed the truck but was able to grab the board's slippery wooden tail as he drifted by.

"Hold on!" Cale yelled.

The water pushed JT to the side of the wall as he dangled from the end of the board. Just as his hand slipped from the tail end, he managed to grab one of the rungs on the grate. With all his might, JT held on to the rusty metal.

"Pull me up, pull me up!" Toby yelled, still hanging upside down. Cale and Skylar immediately hoisted him back up to the top of the wall.

JT was able to get one of his feet on one of the horizontal bars of the grate and pull himself out of the water. From there, Cale and Toby grabbed an arm each, dug their heels into the edge of the bowl, and pulled JT up over the lip, where he fell into a wet, unmoving heap.

Cale looked around at the blank faces of the skaters on the edge of the Sinkhole. Without saying a thing, they all began to scurry, heading to higher ground. It was tough for them to get a foothold; with each climbing footstep, the hill gave way a little bit and chunks of scree went sliding down the hill like mini avalanches. Within a few minutes, however, the entire group had made their way to a small, rocky ridge, where they plunked themselves on the ground. They stared below, fascinated, as the murky, twisting water in the Sinkhole reached full swell.

"I've read about this before," Toby said, panting. "It's called a flash flood. But I had no idea it could happen so fast."

The rest of the guys just looked at Toby blankly, so he continued his explanation. Somewhere deep in the mountains that lay behind them, there had been a rainstorm, perhaps a great distance away. This rainstorm had caused some form of natural dam to break, setting a wall of water loose, heading to the lowest possible point.

"The Sinkhole would have been built for exactly this kind of flood," Toby concluded. "Too bad it's also built perfectly for skateboarding."

"That could have been me," JT said, watching a huge tree branch head into the Sinkhole before being sucked into the tunnel.

"We sure picked the wrong day for a visit, huh?" Ryan said, forcing a few of the guys to laugh a bit.

Cale finally tore his gaze away from the Sinkhole and spotted a trail that led off the ridge they were on.

"Guys, I don't know about you, but I'll bet my mom's wondering where I am by now," he said. He stood up and stretched, then grabbed his belongings and set off along the dusty ridge that seemed to lead back in the direction of the cul-de-sac. "Let's roll."

CHAPTER 18
THIS CREW NEEDS HEROES

It was the first week of August in Drayton and the excitement of what had come to be known as the "Sinkhole incident" had worn off. The town had, just as Cale suspected it would, placed big "NO TRESPASSING" signs all over the place and installed new grates and gates and fencing so that nobody could get within a mile of the once-legendary skate spot.

But it didn't stop the crew from talking about it every chance they could. School was only three weeks away and their ritual of meeting up at the stairs had a new component to it: reliving the incredible moments they'd had that summer. There was also one other topic of conversation that came up: Toby. Even though an ollie down the seven set had eluded him, the rest of the crew had made an incredibly radical decision.

Cale, JT, Skylar, Josh, and Ryan got to the Plaza early and set their plan in motion. They each took a spot in the shadows or behind corners waiting for Toby. They were giddy with excitement.

Toby rolled up just a little after nine-thirty, whistling to himself and holding a giant energy drink

All of a sudden JT's voice came out of nowhere. "Of all the people to save me it had to be you, Toby."

"JT?" he said, squinting. "Where are you?"

JT stepped out of from behind a concrete pillar. "You saved my life. Did you know that?"

"You'd have done the same for me," Toby said. "At least, I hope you would have."

Cale stepped out from behind another corner. "That kind of bravery makes ollieing down a set of seven stairs seem like child's play."

Toby bit his lip, confused by the ambush.

"What is this?" he asked. "Is this some kind of joke?"

"No joke," JT said.

"Welcome to the Seven Stair Crew," Josh said, as he rolled out from the shadows, flanked by Ryan and Skylar.

"Really?" said Toby. "I'm in?"

"Of course you're in," JT said. "We all took a vote."

Toby's hand shook as he raised his energy drink to his lips. "You guys better not be kidding with me, or I'll kill you."

"We're not kidding," Ryan said.

Placing a hand on Toby's shoulder, Cale looked square into his friend's shining eyes. "This crew needs heroes," he said.

★　　★　　★

A few nights later, Cale was sitting across the dinner table from his mom, when she said something that Cale did not expect.

"So, what are you going to do now that you've found all your dad's old haunts?"

"What?" Cale said, almost choking on his potatoes.

"Well, you found all those old spots your dad used to skate. Now that the game is over, what are your plans?" she asked. "What do you want to do with the rest of your summer?"

"How did you know about what I was — well, what we were — doing?"

"I've been in touch with your dad. He's filled me in on the little game. He's very proud of you."

Cale blushed. "I thought you never wanted to talk to him again. More importantly, I thought you didn't want me talking to him."

Cale's mom picked at her salad. "Well, I get the feeling he's really trying. Which is something I never thought he'd do."

"Okay . . ." Cale said. "So you're all right with the fact I've been in touch with him?"

"He's your father, Cale," she said. "I don't think it's the worst idea if you have a relationship with him. I mean, I can't stop you. Which is why I was asking about your plans for the rest of the summer."

Cale's heart jumped in his chest. "What do you mean?" he asked.

"Well, he'd really like to meet you," she said, her voice wavering. "He even sent money for a return plane ticket."

"What, really?" Cale said, remembering the second envelope that was delivered on the day he got the final package from his father.

"Yes, really," she said. "He's offered to pay for you to fly out to California. He wants you to go for a visit before school starts."

"But Mom," Cale said, "is this really okay with you? I won't do it, unless you think it's fine. Mom?"

"The weird thing," she said, sniffling, "is that I want you to go." She teared up a bit and Cale went over to hug her.

"I won't go if you don't want me to, Mom. Really. Just tell me."

"No," she said. "It'll be good for you." She straightened up. "But no longer than one week. I'm the one booking the tickets, so I'll make sure of it." She wagged her finger jokingly and brushed away the last of her tears.

★   ★   ★

That night, Cale lay in bed, staring into the darkness. His mind shuffled images restlessly, like a deck of cards, or a stack of photos he couldn't slow down.

He saw flashes of his crew, his mom, Angie, the Orphans, Toby. His mind's eye lingered long on an image of his father.

He pulled the sheets off his body and slid out of bed. Flipping on his desk lamp, he grabbed a pen from the top drawer and ripped a piece of lined paper from a binder. He began to write. At first he scribbled down just words, small phrases, jumbles of thoughts. But the words began to take a shape and form.

I've gotten quite a few letters this summer. Maybe it's my turn to write one. Sorry there's no map or pictures included. Just my thoughts and feelings. To be honest, I don't know if I'll ever send this . . .

I've also learned a lot this summer. I've learned to

push myself and not to be scared about what might happen, even if that means I might get hurt.

I've learned that you are better off with a crew supporting you rather than being on your own.

I've learned that heroes do exist, and they aren't who you think they are going to be.

I've also learned about the Empire. It was about finding new parts of Drayton, places I had never been. I guess this town isn't as boring and empty as I thought! Was the whole "quest" just a game? At first I figured you were just testing me to see if I could follow the clues properly — stepping into your past, seeing the world through your eyes, finding hidden places so they would become special to both of us. I set out thinking that. But now I know it is not that simple. I realize it was a chance to learn so much more about you — how rough you had it and how you were always searching. I was searching too, and I wasn't sure what I was going to find.

Some people have made me feel like I can't count on you. That you can't be trusted. But I have my own opinion. The fact is, you kept your word with me. You kept sending letters. Maybe you're trying to change. I don't know.

But I'm willing to find out.

Cale, stopped writing, interlaced his hands, and stretched. It felt good to write his thoughts down. As he read the letter over two more times, he fiddled with Angie's St. Christopher medal around his neck. Then he picked up the pen again and scribbled some more.

I also think that while I was out there, finding the Empire, I wasn't just finding out about you or finding new parts of the world.

I was finding new parts of me.

As he wrote the final line, he realized that he hadn't been writing the letter only to his dad. He'd been writing it to himself as well.

He folded the paper in half and then in half again, making a little square. He slid it under the heavy base of his desk lamp next to his passport and plane tickets, then he switched off the light and slipped back into bed.

Cale's mind was clear, and as he drifted off to sleep, he knew that he was ready for whatever was coming next.

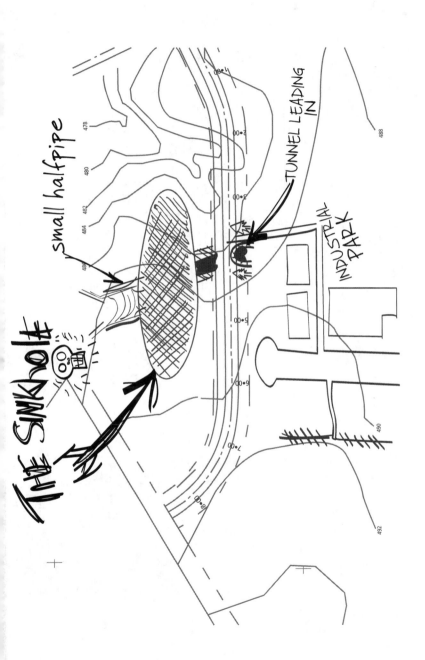

THE SEVEN STAIR CREW

Don't miss the first two books in the trilogy!

It's spring break and Cale Finch's only plans involve skateboarding and hanging out with the guys in the Seven Stair Crew. It's a week-long adventure filled with gnarly tricks, late-night rides, rival crews, and a Street Kings skate contest. Through it all, Cale has to prove that he's got what it takes to roll with the best.

Cale Finch and the Seven Stair Crew are shooting a skate video featuring all their gnarly tricks. They are stoked when Mark Skinner, a local skate legend, offers to help. But then tragedy strikes after a late-night adventure. It will take all Cale's strength and courage to carry on and unite the skateboarding community.

BUY BOTH BOOKS ONLINE AT
lorimer.ca